Pride Publishing books by L.M. Somerton

Single Books
Mountain Rescue
Black Dog
The Portrait
Stroke Rate
Chemical Bonds
Testing Lysander
Owned by the Sea

The Wyverns
Mantrap
Deathtrap
Rattrap
Sand Trap
Steel Trap

Tales from The Edge
Reaching the Edge
Living on the Edge
Dancing on the Edge
A Double-Edged Sword
Rough Around the Edges
Scorched Edges
Driven to the Edge
Binding the Edges
Edging Closer

Investigating Love
Rasputin's Kiss
Evil's Embrace
Tarot's Love

Warlocks
Elemental Love
Elemental Hope
Elemental Faith

The Retreat
Serving Him
Trusting Him
Finding Him

Fairground Attractions
Ghost Train
Merry-Go-Round
Helter Skelter

Treasure Trove Antiques
The Lucky Cat
The Gilded Mirror

Anthologies
Racing Hearts: Keeping the Luck
His Rules: Tagging Mackenzie
Hard Evidence: Secret's Hold

Treasure Trove Antiques

THE POISON BOTTLE

L.M. SOMERTON

The Poison Bottle
ISBN # 978-1-80250-966-3
©Copyright L.M. Somerton 2022
Cover Art by Kelly Martin ©Copyright July 2022
Interior text design by Claire Siemaszkiewicz
Pride Publishing

Published in 2022 by Pride Publishing, United Kingdom.

Pride Publishing is an imprint of Totally Entwined Group Limited.

THE POISON
BOTTLE

Dedication

To my American consultant, we truly are two nations divided by a common language. You made this book so much better.

Chapter One

Landry Carran gave his ass a rub and grinned at the resulting ache. His boyfriend and Dom, Detective Gage Roskam, had delivered a stupendous spanking less than an hour earlier, and Landry was still glowing — physically and mentally. He gave a happy jig then bounced down the stairs from the apartment he shared with Gage to Treasure Trove Antiques, which occupied the ground floor of the building and was his place of gainful-ish employment. The two cups of strong coffee and bowl of sugar-laden cereal that he'd had for breakfast ensured his current energetic state would last for at least an hour, which was when his best friend and assistant, Petey Templeton, would join him. Landry didn't usually have to open the store alone, but Petey had finally given in to a nagging toothache and had an early dental appointment.

"Such a wuss," Landry muttered. "Can't believe I had to bribe him to go." *Worth it though. An assistant who doesn't want to eat baked goods is no use to me at all. That globe he had his eye on was a small price to pay.* Petey had a thing for maps and had fallen in love with a battered globe that dated back to the nineteen seventies. It was about as accurate as a Fox News report, but Petey liked finding the mistakes. Landry had gotten so fed up of Petey whining about his tooth, he'd promised Petey the globe if he put aside his phobia of dentists and got it taken care of. Landry had also persuaded Carson, Petey's boyfriend, to act as escort and make sure he made his appointment. Carson had been happy to help because, as he'd put it, "*a boyfriend who cries when you kiss him does not boost a man's confidence.*"

Bopping and humming as he went, Landry unlocked the door between the building's stairwell and the store. As he entered the cavernous space, piled high with antiques and collectables, he took a deep breath. The familiar scent of beeswax polish, old wood and leather always settled him and put him in the right frame of mind for a day at work. He moved around the store, turning on an eclectic mix of lighting—mainly old lamps that were for sale because his boss, Mr. Lao, insisted that they were more attractive to potential buyers when lit. Of course that meant that whenever they sold one, a corner of the store would be in the dark until Mr. Lao obtained a new one to replace it, but Landry didn't mind because part of Treasure Trove Antiques' charm was its nooks and crannies. He knew the stock inside and out but loved seeing the wonder on customers' faces when they spotted something unique or unusual hidden behind an aging armoire or balancing on top of a bookcase stuffed with rare tomes. He glanced around, checking that all was as he'd left it the previous evening. Everything was as it should be. Not that there was any reason for him to think otherwise, but there had been an incident with a mouse once when somehow, the tiny rodent had set up home in a basket of vintage tablecloths and had nibbled a hole through two of them before he was spotted. It had taken a humane trap and enough peanut butter to feed a raccoon, let alone a mouse, to catch the beast, so Landry was constantly on the lookout for any sign of critters in the store.

He grabbed the long pole he needed to lift the security shutter into place then went back into the hall. He left the building then crossed the yard to the alley gate. After his usual fight with the padlock, he rounded the corner of the building to the street. His friend Prisha, whose dad owned the Eastern Emporium opposite Treasure Trove, was outside brushing down the sidewalk with hot soapy water. Landry gave her a wave before jogging across the road.

"Hey, Prisha, what's going down?"

"What came *up*, more like." She grimaced. "Somebody deposited the contents of their stomach on the sidewalk last night. So gross."

Landry wrinkled his nose. "Better you than me, especially first thing in the morning."

"Hey, if you want to do a girl a favor, I'd be happy to hand over the broom."

"No can do." Landry grinned. "Petey's at the dentist so I have to open on my own this morning. Gotta go before hordes of voracious customers start beating on the security shutter."

"Yeah, I can see where they're lining up around the block." Prisha went back to brushing. "I'll come over on my break later. You can buy me a coffee."

"Deal. Have a good morning." Landry skipped back across the street, managing not to trip over his pole. He had less trouble opening the security shutter than closing it because he didn't have to get the hook on the end of his pole through the tiny D-ring that allowed him to draw it down. It was way above his head and like trying to thread a needle while standing on the deck of a pitching boat. Opening up just meant using the pole to push the shutter back into place once he'd released the padlock that locked it to a concealed ring in the sidewalk. A padlock that was no longer in place.

Landry frowned. He distinctly remembered snapping it shut the night before because he'd scraped a knuckle doing it. "Fuckety-fuck. What the heck is going on?"

There was no sign of vandalism or any other damage to the shutter. Landry shrugged, slipped the pole into place then pushed. The shutter rolled up of its own accord, only needing a shove for the last couple of feet. Landry unhooked the pole then gaped. In the recessed store doorway was a person, huddled in a ball, facing away from him.

"What on earth…? Hey, padlock thief, you can't stay there." He groped in his pocket for a few dollars. "Go get yourself some breakfast."

Whoever it was didn't move. With a sick feeling in the pit of his stomach, Landry propped his pole against the store window then leaned over his visitor. He touched his shoulder, gave it a little shake and the man rolled toward him.

"Holy fuck!" He was dead. Completely and absolutely deceased. Blood stained the front of the beige trench coat he wore. There was a blue tinge to his skin and his eyes were open, staring.

Landry danced back a few steps as he stared at the corpse. "No, no, no… This is not good for business. I

mean, poor guy, but why *my* shop doorway?" His cell
was inside so he turned and waved frantically at Prisha
who dropped her broom before running across the
street. "Call 911! I found a body."

Prisha, who was always good in a crisis, did a quick
turn and rocketed into the Eastern Emporium. She was
soon back with her dad at her side.

"The cops are on their way," she said, putting an
arm around Landry's now shaking shoulders. "You
should call Gage. Here, use this." She handed over her
cell, but Landry's hands were trembling too much to
punch in the number. Prisha grabbed it back. "Tell me
the number. I'll call him for you."

Landry reeled it off without thinking. He couldn't
tear his eyes away from the dead body and his
bloodstained clothing.

"Gage, it's Prisha. I'm here with Landry and… Yes,
he's fine but the dead guy he just found behind the
security shutter isn't looking so good."

"What?" Landry heard Gage's yell even from where
he was standing. He took the cell back.

"Can you come home, Sir?" Landry used the
honorific without thinking, defaulting to his role as
Gage's submissive rather than his boyfriend in his
stressed state. "There's a b-b-b…body. A real-life body,
I mean it's a dead body but it's real. An actual genuine,
honest to God, not breathing, corpse. And it's in the
shop porch blocking the door and there's blood. Gage,
why is there a dead person in my shop doorway?"
Tears welled in Landry's eyes and he sniffled.

"I'm not really in a position to answer that question
yet, love. Stay put. Sancha and I are on our way. Who's
there with you?"

"Petey's at the dentist and Mr. Lao isn't here but Prisha and her dad have come over."

"Stay with them. I mean it, Landry. You are not to go anywhere on your own."

"Not going anywhere," Landry mumbled as Gage ended the call. "How can I go anywhere when there are dead people?"

"It's one dead person, Landry, not a massacre."

"Where there's one, there might be others. That's logical." Landry glanced around in case more corpses littered the place.

Prisha gave him a comforting hug. She and her dad had been joined by the guy who had been cleaning windows at the café next door to Treasure Trove and the crew of a passing garbage truck. The manager of the café arrived with a tray of coffees and a plate piled with Danish pastries.

"Someone came into the café and said there's a body out here. I know it doesn't seem appropriate," she said, "but a hot drink and something sweet will take your mind off what's going on, Landry. It'll help with the shock."

"Thanks, Mary." Landry discovered that shoving a cherry Danish in his mouth made all the difference. A new infusion of sugar and caffeine into his system helped him see things in a more clinical light and stop thinking about how on earth a dead man had gotten behind the security shutter. "The padlock," he said, spraying crumbs. "When I came to lift the shutter earlier, the padlock was gone. I wonder where it is."

The small crowd started searching up and down the sidewalk and it wasn't long before there was a shout from one of the garbage crew. "Found it!" Landry, coffee in hand, walked over to look at where the guy was pointing. The padlock lay in the gutter, partly covered by a discarded banana skin.

"I guess we should leave it where it is," Landry said, "in case of fingerprints."

"That's right. I'm Elton." The garbage guy held out his hand, which Landry shook, hoping that his fingers wouldn't be crushed in the process. Elton was built like a linebacker.

"Nice to meet you, Elton. Shame it couldn't have been under better circumstances."

"You'd be surprised how many bodies we come across in our line of work," Elton said, sounding philosophical. "We get training on what not to do when it comes to possible evidence. We were about to empty the dumpsters along the street when we saw what was going on, so we'll leave them until the cops get here. They may want to keep the contents to search through for clues."

"Well, I never thought of that." Landry was fascinated.

"I don't suppose antique selling is a job that gets you involved in much crime," Elton said.

Landry thought about the last few months, the adventures he and Gage had had, first with his lucky cat and then the gilded mirror. "No, not really. Old stuff is tame."

"I wonder if there are any pastries left." Elton ambled toward the café where Mary was eyeing him like a piece of prime beef. Landry shook his head. "People sure do meet under the strangest of circumstances," he muttered, watching Elton get coy and stutter in front of Mary.

Sirens announced the arrival of the cops and not long afterward, Gage's Jeep screeched to a halt next to a patrol car. He and Sancha jumped out and while Sancha went over to the uniforms, Gage headed straight for Landry.

"Again? Really?" He drew Landry into a tight hug.

"So not my fault," Landry mumbled into the hard planes of Gage's chest. "It's not like I have a sign up saying 'leave your dead bodies here', is it?"

"You attract trouble like a magnet."

Landry nuzzled against Gage's body. He could feel the warmth of his skin through his shirt and smell the gel he'd used in the shower that morning. "Do not."

"Do so."

"Someone cut off the padlock. It's in the gutter over there. They must have lifted the grill, dumped the body in the porch then pulled it down again."

"I want you to go sit in the café," Gage said, "while Sancha and I get the investigation started."

"Will you be assigned the case?" Landry asked.

"If the captain doesn't think I have a conflict of interest, it's quite likely." Gage steered Landry toward the café. He gestured for Prisha to come over and asked her to stay with Landry.

Landry didn't want to leave the safety of Gage's arms but knew he had to let him do his job. Once he'd settled at a table in the café with Prisha next to him, he took a deep breath and eased some of his tension with a roll of his shoulders. He slurped his coffee. "Here we go again."

"Are you ready for another adventure?" Prisha asked.

"It's not like I had a choice the first time, or the second. Hopefully this will amount to nothing." Landry didn't need Prisha's skeptical expression or his own gut feeling to tell him that amounting to nothing was the least likely outcome of the morning's events. He wondered if impending doom merited another pastry.

Chapter Two

With Prisha egging him on, Landry worked his way through two vanilla lattes and had moved on to a hot chocolate with whipped cream and marshmallows by the time Gage pushed his way into the café. He made straight for the table.

"And that's my signal to leave," Prisha said, getting to her feet.

"You don't have to go, Prisha," Gage said, giving her a hug. "I'd guess you've been holding a certain someone together this morning."

"He's glued together with caffeine and sugar, but I really do need to go. Pop's been on his own in the store too long already, and he has a tendency to light the most revolting combination of incense sticks you've ever had the misfortune to smell when I'm not there to stop him. You know where I am if you need more girl hugs, Landry. Please don't find any more bodies."

"The woman talks sense," Gage said. "You should listen to her because you sure as hell don't pay me any mind."

"Do so."

"Not unless I have you tied to the bed, you don't." Prisha made a run for it, giggling as she went. "And you have a whipped-cream mustache," Gage added.

Landry attempted a sultry expression as he ran his tongue around his lips. "Yum, you said whipped."

"Juvenile."

"Yes, Sir. Selective obedience makes for an interesting life."

"It sure does. The ME's people are about to remove the body, Lan. I need you to come take a look to see if you recognize him."

"Do I have to?" Landry gripped his mug of chocolate harder.

"No, but it would be helpful. I'll be right there with you. There's no need to be scared." Gage gave Landry's shoulder a squeeze and Landry leaned against him.

"I'm not scared but what if I *do* know him? I didn't focus on his face earlier—I was too shocked to concentrate."

"If you do, you do. It's not going to change by avoiding it. You should get it over with."

"That's such a Gage thing to say." Landry pushed his mug away then got to his feet. He found a few dollars to leave the server, slapping the bills on the table a little harder than was necessary. "Okay, let's go." He still dragged his feet as he waved to Mary and followed Gage out of the café onto the street.

Landry had always thought the area had a nice, friendly vibe, but now, all that had changed. The cop cars, the small crowd of onlookers that had gathered and the crime scene tape that surrounded the area in front of the store all contributed to an oppressive, sinister atmosphere. An involuntary shiver ran down

Landry's spine. He ducked beneath the tape that Gage lifted for him then approached the store with some trepidation.

"You're going a bit blue," Gage observed. "Why were you outside without a coat?"

"Because I was supposed to be out here for five minutes lifting the shutter, not standing in the street staring at corpses. It was warm in the café but it's frigid out here." Landry fixed his gaze on the body bag resting on top of a gurney a few feet away.

"Point taken."

Gage took off his jacket then placed it around Landry's shoulders. Landry shrugged into it. It was far too big and only the tips of his fingers poked from the sleeves, but it was warm and smelled of Gage. "Thanks. Sorry. I shouldn't have snapped at you. I'm a bit freaked."

"Snap all you like, love. This will only take a minute. Then, if the crime scene techs have finished, everything will be cleared up and you'll be able to open the store like usual."

Landry squared his shoulders. "I'm ready. Let's do this." He put on a brave face but was glad of Gage's presence next to him, rock steady and certain. They stood next to the gurney while a staffer from the ME's office unzipped the body bag a short way.

"You'll need to have your eyes open to stand any chance of identifying him," Gage said, his tone betraying his amusement.

Landry kept them shut. "Is there blood? Is it gruesome?"

"Not at all. He could be sleeping."

Landry opened one eye to be on the safe side, but Gage was telling the truth.

"Oh! He does look kinda peaceful. You're sure he's dead, right?"

"He has seven stab wounds, Landry. They're just in body parts you can't see."

Landry gave Gage a long, slow stare. "You didn't have to tell me that!"

"Do you know him or not?"

"Not…I mean, no. Never seen him before. Oh, there's Mr. Lao! Don't let him kill me, Gage." Landry gave his boss a wave. "One body a day is enough for anyone but opening late is a felony in his book."

Gage gestured to the cop standing at the crime scene tape to let Mr. Lao through, and he ducked beneath the ribbon before running over to join them.

"It's not my fault!" Landry got in before anyone else could say a word.

Gage drew him close. "This time he's right, Mr. L. I'm afraid there was a body outside the store this morning."

"Not just outside," Landry said. "Behind the security shutter! I'm gonna be taking the cost of hair dye out of the petty cash because I gained a few white strands this morning, I swear. Also, bleach. Gallons of the stuff to swab out the porch."

"Always with the drama…should I take a look at the dead man, Gage?"

"Sure, I'd only have to come back with a picture anyways."

Mr. Lao proved to be a lot more stoic than Landry. He took one quick glance at the dead man and nodded. "I know him."

Landry gaped. "You do?"

"You should too, Landry. You've met him, though it was a while ago."

"I have?" Landry took another look at the body, but the man's face didn't seem familiar. He shook his head. "I don't recall him at all."

Gage gave a nod and the ME's people zipped the body bag shut before levering the gurney into the back of their wagon. "Let's go inside. Mr. Lao can enlighten us once I get Sancha to join us. Go on in, I won't be a second."

Landry, his head hanging, scuffed his feet as he followed Mr. Lao down the side alley and through the courtyard into the back of the building. The front door had to be unlocked from the inside, so he did that while Mr. Lao made himself a mug of pungent green tea.

"You want tea, Landry?" Mr. Lao shouted.

"Pond slime," Landry muttered. "No thank you." He headed for the counter at the back of the store. "I've had too many drinks already this morning, Mr. L, so I'll have to say no just this once."

Mr. Lao put his mug on the cash desk. "My hearing is as good as ever, young man. Your beverage appreciation is as lacking as always. I'll be mentioning your cheek to Gage."

"If it looks like pond slime, smells like pond slime and tastes like pond slime…it *is* pond slime! I'm just calling it like I see it."

"Do you try pond slime often?"

"Every time I taste tea!"

"What's this about slime?" Sancha walked up to them. She pulled an elaborately carved chair over to the cash desk then sat with a sigh. "It's good to take the weight off my feet."

"You do look a bit tired," Landry said. "Have you been burning the candle at both ends?"

"I should be so lucky. No, both kids have had a stomach flu and the last two nights have been full of interesting substances coming out of both ends of them."

"Gah! I wish I hadn't asked." Landry fought down a sudden urge to vomit.

Sancha chuckled. "Bringing up kids is harder work than being a detective sometimes."

"So is dealing with Landry," Gage muttered as he joined them.

"Hey, I resemble that remark." Landry batted his lashes at Gage.

"Perhaps we could get back to the small matter of the dead body in the porch," Gage said, producing his notebook.

"Do we have to? I'd rather forget all about it." Landry pouted.

"We do. Put that lip away. I already have the details of how everything unfolded this morning, and Sancha has taken statements from everyone who was around when Landry made his discovery. I've arranged for the dumpsters in the area to be preserved for searching in case someone disposed of a weapon, but on initial inspection, the ME thinks that the killing took place elsewhere. The only blood we found was on the body. So, it's over to you, Mr. Lao. Tell us what you know about the victim."

Mr. Lao took a sip of his tea then cleared his throat. "There's not that much to tell, I'm afraid. His name is Arthur Penton, and he owns Penton's Antiquarium. His main store is on Washington Street, and he has another smaller branch in Olympia. Like most of us dealers, he also has an online presence. He is, or rather was, a bit of a prima donna. He imported most of his stock from Europe and operated at the more expensive end of the market. We had a few business dealings over the years. As a person, I found him affected and rather too pleased with himself, but I have to admit he had an eye for a good quality piece. He specialized in mid-Georgian, English Rococo and Neoclassical furniture and had a particular interest in Chippendale."

"I remember now," exclaimed Landry. "He came in here once to look at a washstand you picked up on a buying trip to Vancouver. He turned up his nose at everything else but had a buyer ready and waiting for the washstand, so didn't even negotiate very much on the price."

"Knowing, no doubt, that he'd still make a substantial profit," Mr. Lao said.

"I wouldn't have known him if I'd passed him in the street," Landry said.

"No reason why you should. It was a brief meeting, and I was the one that dealt with him. From what I remember your role was to carry the piece out to his van."

"That's right! And the lackey he had with him was far too self-important to help."

Gage finished scribbling on his pad. "When was the last time you saw him in person, Mr. Lao?"

"That's easy. Three months ago, there was a dinner for the regional antiques association. I attended and so did Penton. We weren't seated at the same table, but I did say hello to him in passing. He made some comment about business being booming then moved on to talk to more influential people. I can give you the contact details of the organizers, who should be able to send you a list of everyone who attended. It's a regular, annual thing. Lots of well-lubricated schmoozing, barely edible food and a charity raffle where everyone is expected to contribute a prize." He stared into the depths of his mug. "I haven't seen him since. Before that, I think about six months earlier, I bought a couple of pieces from him that he wanted to move on to make space for new stock but that was a rarity. His stuff is usually too expensive."

"Is there anything else you think might be useful for us to know?" Gage asked.

Mr. Lao shook his head. "Nothing comes to mind, but I'll call if I think of anything."

There was a commotion at the door and Landry's store assistant and best friend, Petey, pushed his way inside.

Gage strolled down the aisle to reassure the cop who was trying to block Petey's path that it was okay to let him into the store.

"Big meany!" Petey gave the cop an appraising examination before licking his lips.

"That's enough of that," Gage reprimanded. "Don't make me tell Carson about you eyeing up men in uniform."

Petey's eyes widened, and he scuttled down the aisle toward Landry who greeted him with a laugh and a hug. "You're shameless. He is hot though."

"Isn't he just. What's going on, Landry? There are cops everywhere, bits of crime scene tape and far too many people in Mary's for this time of the day." Petey's speech was a bit slurred.

"Have you been drinking, Petey?" Mr. Lao asked.

"I've been to the dentist. I had to have a filling and that meant lots of big needles and anesthetic. Half my head is numb and speaking feels weird. Am I dribbling?" He dabbed his mouth. "I keep feeling like there's drool running down my chin."

"Only what the hotty cop generated. Where's Carson?" Landry asked.

Petey scrubbed the back of his hand across his mouth. "You're a big fat liar and he had to go into work. Someone called in sick so he's covering. Is anyone going to tell me what's going on? Sancha, you make more sense than any of this bunch. What have I missed?"

Landry gave him a shove. "Hey, I'm your best friend, not Sancha. You were lucky you had to be at the dentist this morning. I found a body."

"You found a what now?"

"Body. Dead person. No longer breathing. Behind the security shutter when I went to open up."

"Why was there a dead body behind the security shutter, Landry?"

Landry rolled his eyes. "How in the ever-loving heck am I supposed to know? I didn't put it there. Sancha and Gage have to find out. Mr. Lao knew him. It was Arthur Penton from The Antiquarium."

"Wow. I mean, I didn't know him but I've heard of the place. I should call Carson, he's bound to hear about this and he'll be worried."

"And why would he be worried, Petey? It was me who found the body. You're supposed to be my best buddy. You should be comforting me or at least offering to fetch coffee." Landry pouted until he caught Gage's eye. "But of course you should call Carson first."

Gage shook his head. "Well, you're all set to open the store now."

"What if whoever killed poor Mr. Penton comes back?" Landry asked, not wanting to come across as nervous, but needing reassurance.

"Highly unlikely," Gage said. "I wouldn't be leaving you here if I thought there was a chance that you'd be in any danger, you know that."

"I do… But…"

"I'll be checking in on you by phone at least once an hour." Gage drew Landry into a firm hug. "And if time allows I'll call in on my break, okay? Murderers aren't in the habit of returning to body dumps."

Landry shuddered. "Body dump sounds so… messy." He didn't want Gage to let go of him. He was tempted to do his best impression of a limpet, but Gage had to work, and he had the store to open.

Gage extricated himself. "Are you going to be here this morning, Mr. Lao?"

"I only stopped in to take a look over the stock situation. I have buying trips planned and need to have a rough list in my head of the kind of things I should be looking for. I can stay as long as the boys need me though. I don't have anything else on today."

Petey bounced on the spot. He loved Mr. Lao because the old man treated him like a grandson and let him get away with murder.

"I can see what you're thinking, Petey. Don't forget who's the store manager and your boss." Landry put his hands on his hips and tried to look stern. "You have dust bunnies to hunt down."

"So mean. I've been traumatized by a dentist scarier than that nut job in *Little Shop of Horrors*. You should be nice to me."

"Dead guy trumps dentist, Petey." Landry licked the tip of his finger and made a number one sign in the air.

"Mr. Lao, good luck with wrangling these two and be assured that the Seattle PD will turn a blind eye should you feel the need to apply a ruler to a passing posterior," Gage said.

Landry and Petey gasped in unison as Mr. Lao gave Gage a thumbs-up. Sancha heaved herself up from her seat then gave Landry's shoulder a sympathetic pat. "He'll make it up to you later, sweetie," she whispered.

"He'd better, or I'll be rescinding his cuddle privileges. Make sure you give him all the worst paperwork to do."

"Don't I always?" Sancha ruffled Petey's hair, winked at Mr. Lao, then followed Gage who was heading for the door.

"I heard every word of that," Gage grumbled.

"You were meant to," Sancha retorted.

Landry waggled his fingers at Gage then turned to Petey. "As soon as you get the chance," he whispered, "take that old wooden ruler out of the drawer under the cash register and hide it somewhere."

"Deal." They high fived.

Landry turned to Mr. Lao. "Time for us to do some research into Penton's Antiquarium, don't you think?"

"You read my mind. You operate that confounded computer. I'll supervise."

Chapter Three

That evening, Gage was late getting home. Landry kept a plate warm for him and waited up, curled into a corner of the couch. He'd showered, changed into his warmest jammies and a pair of fluffy socks then dragged the comforter from the bed into the living room so that he could burrow beneath it. Gage had texted that he'd be home around midnight but showed up ten minutes before that looking rumpled and drawn. Landry poked his nose out of his nest.

"That's lucky."

"What is?" Gage managed a soft smile even though he was obviously dead on his feet.

"You made it back before the Cinderella hour."

"And the significance of that is?" Shucking his jacket, Gage kicked off his shoes before working his way beneath the comforter. He pulled Landry onto his lap. Nuzzling his hair, he took a deep breath. "You smell of…chocolate. I'm afraid to ask but why does your hair smell of chocolate?"

"Free shampoo sample from the mall and the Cinderella hour is when I turn from a gorgeous prince into a frog."

"I think you're mixing up your fairy tales."

"Yes, but I've always thought that a glass shoe would be excruciatingly uncomfortable whereas you'll have to kiss me after midnight to turn me back into a prince."

"Sound logic. If I weren't so tired, my anticipation level would be off the scale."

"You want food? I saved you something."

"I could eat. You might have to prod me to stop me face-planting in the plate though."

"It's mac and cheese, so that would be so icky." Landry fetched Gage's meal then kept a close eye on him while he ate. He did *not* want to be picking soggy noodles out of Gage's hair.

"Thanks, love. That was great. I'm going to take a quick shower, then fall into bed."

"You need me to make sure you don't drown in there?" Landry asked as he headed to the kitchen to clean up the dishes.

"Thoughtful, but no. I think I can make it." Gage's wry tone made Landry smile.

With the kitchen clean and tidy, Landry hauled the comforter back to the bedroom. He bashed the pillows until they were nice and plump then stripped off his jammies. Gage liked to sleep naked, and Landry had no problem with skin-to-skin contact. Gage was always warm and never complained when Landry stuck his cold feet on him. Of course, he usually threatened a spanking but that didn't deter Landry. He liked spankings—a lot. Tonight though, Landry wanted his Dom to be warm, cozy and to get a decent night's sleep. A new case was always frantic to start with and Landry had gotten used to Gage's unsociable hours over the time they'd been together.

Landry had just snuggled beneath the covers when Gage, a towel slung around his hips, strolled into the room. Landry willed the towel to fall. Firm pecs and strong thighs were drool-worthy, but the best bits were still covered.

"I toweled my hair but it's still a bit damp," Gage muttered.

"And very sexy. Love that tousled look. You want the hairdryer?"

"No, I'll deal. It's warm enough in here." Gage dropped the towel then did a long, slow stretch.

Landry gaped. "How do you expect me to sleep when you do that right in front of me?"

"What?" Gage got into bed, grinning. "I don't know what you're talking about."

"Flaunting that sexy bod. No fair."

"Stop pouting. I saw you wishing that towel away." Gage yawned. "Don't think about denying it, I know you."

"I didn't say a word, how did you know?"

"The lustful expression on your very cute face. Come here." He pulled Landry closer, turning him so that he became the little spoon. "Much better."

Landry gave a happy sigh. He adored having Gage's cock wedged against his ass. "Good night." He didn't get a response because Gage was already snoring.

* * * *

"Landry. Lan!"

Landry sat bolt upright with a yelp. He was soaked in sweat and a scream froze on his lips. "Gage?" His voice shook.

"Right here. You were having a bad dream."

"Oh God, I'm sorry. What time is it?" Disorientation rode Landry hard.

"About three." Gage wrapped his arm around Landry's trembling shoulders.

"You've had less than three hours' sleep. I'm so sorry. I kept seeing his face, Penton's that is, and a bloody knife. Someone was plunging it into Penton's body over and over again. He was jerking and his eyes... The terror." Landry gave a strangled sob.

"I thought you were coping a little too well with what happened this morning. That clever mind of yours got busy as soon as you were asleep, didn't it?"

"Apparently." Landry sighed. "Mr. Lao and I were on the computer, researching Penton's business on and off for part of the day. I guess he was foremost in my mind. I'm so sorry, Gage, you need your sleep."

"So do you. You want some hot chocolate?"

"That sounds good. I'm gonna grab a shower real quick, I'm all sweaty and gross."

After freshening up and drinking the mug of chocolate that Gage provided, Landry felt much better. "If I go back to sleep, is it just going to happen again?"

"I won't let it," Gage growled.

"I don't think even your Dommy-ness stretches to controlling my dreams," Landry murmured, but he let Gage arrange him so that he was on his side, one arm slung over Gage's chest and a leg across his thighs. Gage rested a hand on the small of Landry's back. "I have you. You're safe with me, and I will take it as a personal affront if you have another nightmare."

Landry giggled. "Yes, Sir. I promise to dream of fluffy clouds and rainbows, nothing else."

"I should think so." Gage's hand drifted south to rest on Landry's ass, and Landry drifted back to sleep with a broad smile fixed to his face.

Even though the rest of the night proved to be much more restful, Landry did *not* want to get up the following morning. Gage was just as reticent and stayed in bed much longer than he would usually, declaring that he'd be no use to the case if he went into work half-asleep. Landry made them both bowls of porridge laced with honey because he wanted Gage to have a decent meal that would keep him going until he remembered to eat again. He resolved to text him at lunchtime as an additional reminder.

On second thought, I'll text Sancha. She's much more sensible and she'll force-feed him if she needs to.

They danced around each other getting ready, then Gage treated Landry to a lingering kiss before he left. As the door slammed, Landry brought his fingers to his tingling lips and smiled. He wondered how long it would be before they had time to engage in more strenuous morning activities again. "More research for me today. The sooner this case gets solved, the sooner I get sexy times with Gage and if that's not motivation, I don't know what is." With a few bedroom scenarios in mind, he bounced down the stairs to find Petey waiting in the hall.

"I thought you might like me to raise the shutters this morning," Petey said. "After yesterday… You know…"

Landry welled up. "That's so sweet of you!"

Petey blushed and shrugged. "You'd do the same for me." He grabbed the pole that he needed to lift the shutter then headed outside. Landry unlocked the door from the hall into the store then made his way to the cash desk to sort out the register. He cast a few nervous glances toward the front of the store until the shutter creaked upward. He took the lack of screaming as a good sign and strolled down the aisle to turn over the closed sign. Outside, Petey waved at him and gestured at the empty porch. Landry gave him a thumbs-up. One dead body that week was more than enough. He made some exaggerated hand gestures to signal Petey that he was in need of coffee, then realized that he could have just opened the door. He unlocked it then pulled it open.

"Why are you waving your arms around like a demented octopus?" Petey asked. "We've just opened so why in the world would you think that I wouldn't realize that you're in need of coffee? You're always in need of coffee."

"I had a disturbed night, okay? I'm all confuddled. I do want coffee but nothing to eat, thanks. I made porridge for breakfast and I'm really full."

"There has to be a joke in there somewhere about Goldilocks and the one bear."

"Gage isn't a bear. I mean, he has a hairy chest and lots of muscles but… Oh my God, he *is* a bear. A baby bear. That sounds kind of cute."

"More like a full-on raging grizzly," Petey quipped. "But you as Goldilocks, that I can see."

"I don't like the direction this conversation is taking, not before coffee anyway. Get round to the café and while you're there, ask Mary if she got the hot garbage guy's number."

"Hot garbage guy? Have you been withholding gossip from me?"

"There was a lot going on yesterday so pardon me if I didn't remember to pass on every single detail. Besides, you were too busy texting Carson all day to focus on quality gossip. Bring me life-sustaining liquid and I'll fill you in."

Petey thrust the shutter pole at Landry then flounced next door to the café. Landry went back inside Treasure Trove, chuckling. His friend could be the biggest drama queen when he wanted to be.

Landry puttered around until Petey got back with his extra-large, extra-hot vanilla latte, then the two of them settled behind the cash desk. Landry's first sip of his drink generated a satisfied sigh. "So good. I'll buy the next round."

"Mary went bright red when I mentioned hot garbage guy. She said they have a date on Saturday night. He has tickets for the ballet. Apparently he's a big fan and so's she. Seems like a match made in heaven to me. So how did they meet, and how come your sticky fingers are involved?"

"My fingers are not sticky, thank you very much. The hot garbage guy is called Elton. He and his crew were working the street when I found the body, and they stopped to help. Elton was the one who found the missing padlock that whoever dumped the body had tossed away. He hung around because he knew that the cops might want the contents of all the dumpsters so he made sure another crew wouldn't collect them. Mary was supplying everyone with drinks and pastries and that's how they met. That girl has game. She couldn't have made her attraction more obvious. Poor Elton didn't stand a chance. Mind you, he bears a remarkable resemblance to Bobby Wagner, so she has excellent taste."

"I didn't know you had any interest in the Seahawks."

"I don't know one end of a football from the other, you know that doesn't stop me looking at the pretty players though."

"Fair enough, though Wagner isn't with them now, I heard he's going to the Rams."

"And now you've lost me." Landry scanned the store. "Some corners of this place are looking a bit sparse. I hope Mr. Lao is out acquiring new stock. We've sold quite a few of the bigger pieces recently."

"The film people doing that period drama did us a solid favor taking those two triple wardrobes. I swear I expected to find the doorway to Narnia through the back of one of those."

"Wouldn't that be fantastic? Not Narnia specifically but having a secret doorway to another world. That would be fun."

"It so would. Mind you, Carson transports me to other worlds quite effectively every night." Petey grinned. "Last night he decided I needed my mind taken off dead bodies. By the time he was done, I couldn't even string a sentence together."

"You're lucky. Gage was exhausted when he got in and then I had a nightmare and woke him up. I could have done with a bit of pre-sleep distraction too."

"Will he be working the case? He's always stupid busy when he and Sancha start something new."

"As far as I know. He wondered if there might be a conflict of interest, but his only involvement in Treasure Trove is me and the body was found outside, not in the store. I'd say he's in the best position to investigate, not the worst."

"So, are you going to help? I can help too. We worked really well together when it came to solving the case of the gilded mirror."

"Mr. Lao and I did some research into Penton's Antiquarium yesterday while you were stocktaking the rare books, and by the way, I know you were reading more than you were checking prices. We didn't get that far because all those inconvenient customers kept coming in and Mr. Lao seemed to think they were important."

"There were too many for me to handle on my own. Plus Mrs. Schonberger won't let anyone serve her but you," Petey said. "But Mr. L's priorities are all wrong."

"Exactly. That's what I said, but he threatened me with polishing the silver stock if I didn't behave. Honestly, the working conditions here are substandard."

Petey snorted into his drink and Landry collapsed into gales of laughter. The bell over the door chimed as it opened, and a crowd of customers hustled into the store. "Time to earn our pay," Landry said. "We'll get back to the investigation later. Not a word to Carson. He'll tell Gage then neither of us will be sitting comfortably for the next few days."

Petey linked his little finger with Landry's. "Pinky swear."

Landry shook it. "Go do your thing with the customers. We'll start the Scooby stuff when it's quiet."

* * * *

Gage sat at his desk, head in his hands. The start of a headache was building behind his eyes that seemed to be lubricated with damp sand. His in-tray was invisible, concealed beneath a teetering pile of paperwork. A half-drunk mug of cold coffee perched on one corner of the desk, fighting for space with box files, a stapler and a family-sized bag of chips. The desk opposite Gage's was tidy and unoccupied.

"Oy, Roskam. Captain wants you."

Gage peered at his colleague then hauled himself to his feet. He wound between scattered desks, chairs and assorted detectives to reach the room's only office, though it hardly qualified, being not much bigger than the broom closet. Inside, Captain Archibald Henry sat behind his desk. Small and wiry with a nose that credited him with the nickname Bald Eagle, he gestured at Gage to sit. Gage had to shift a pile of folders before perching on the edge of a chair that everyone knew was deliberately designed to be uncomfortable.

"Morning, boss."

"Well the sun fucking rose, so I guess it must be. You got Detective Hernandez's message, I assume?"

Gage nodded and his headache intensified. "She'll be halfway to Mexico by now. Her madre is a fantastic lady. Sancha will do anything for her."

"I've met her mother. She's delightful. Makes unbelievable chilaquiles. However, her gallbladder could have picked a better time to start playing up."

Gage shrugged. "It is what it is." Sancha had left him a long voice message that morning saying that she was on her way to the airport because her mother had to go into the hospital to have her gall bladder removed and needed Sancha to pick up some of her duties at the family's holiday resort for the next two weeks. "She hasn't taken a vacation in an age and since when did you have breakfast with Sancha's mother?"

"I didn't. Sancha brought them in. They went so fast you probably weren't quick enough to snag one. This new case is a sticky one. Penton was a friend of the mayor, and he's blowing smoke up my ass to get a quick result. You need help."

"You're not going to make me break in a new partner now, are you?"

"You should be so lucky. You think I have spare bodies just lying around the place? No, the Brits have an interest in this case. They're sending over some antiques expert, and he'll give you a hand."

"A cop?"

"Not quite. I understand he's an investigator and works as a consultant for the Metropolitan police on and off."

A niggle of doubt poked at a dormant corner of Gage's mind. *It can't be.* "What's his name and when is he arriving?"

"What, no argument? No insisting that you work better alone?"

"I don't. I work better with Sancha but I'll take what I can get. This case is gonna involve a lot of legwork and the caseload around here sucks. Uniform is loaning me a couple of beat officers but the more resources I can get on this the better, especially if the case is going to get attention in slimy places."

"The mayor is not slimy, Roskam. Show some respect. Slippery, self-serving, supercilious — all good words beginning with s. The Brit's name is John Smythe," Captain Henry said. "That's Smythe with a 'y' and an 'e' on the end. He'll be arriving this evening, so you can pick him up from Sea-Tac. You can brief him on the way to his hotel. He'll no doubt be jet lagged to hell and as good as useless, so put him to work tomorrow morning after he's had a decent night's sleep. You look like you could do with one of those yourself."

"Tell me about it."

"Young Landry not sleeping after finding the body?"

"How did you guess?" Gage's boss had met Landry at several work functions and against all the odds had a soft spot for him.

"Because unlike you and me, he's not a cynical old cop. He has a sensitive soul. I hope you're looking after him."

"Why do I get the feeling you like him better than me, boss?"

"That's the detective in you, Gage. Now get out of my office and do some work."

Gage went. He returned to his desk, but only to fetch his jacket. He needed to get some air and he had an antique store to visit.

Penton's Antiquarium had none of the friendly, welcoming vibes that Treasure Trove Antiques gave out. It did have a small parking lot behind the building, which was a mercy in the busy area. Gage inserted his Jeep between a brand-new BMW and a high-end Lexus, repressing the urge to open the Jeep's door a little too wide. Instead, he sucked in his breath and shimmied between the vehicles so as not to cause any damage to their pristine paintwork.

There was a double-width door at the rear of the property, which Gage assumed was used for taking larger pieces of furniture in and out. When he tried it, it was locked and when he peered through the glass, he didn't see any movement inside. He circled the building to the front then crossed the street to get a wider view of the store. There was no denying it had an impressive presence. Broad windows flanked a door furnished with highly polished brass handles. A single piece of furniture was displayed on a raised pedestal behind each window. On one side was an ornate bed with sizeable wooden headboard and footboard, edged with detailed carvings of cherubs. The bed was dressed with gold-edged velvet fabrics in a shade of deep burgundy.

"Bet that's uncomfortable," Gage muttered. In the other window was a French dresser in a dark wood that Gage guessed was mahogany. It stood at least eight feet high and would need a grand room to house it. Gage re-crossed the street to take a closer look in each window. There were small cards describing each piece, but no prices. "If you have to ask, you can't afford it, I suppose." When Gage tried the door, he was a little surprised that it opened. He had expected that the store might be closed out of respect for Penton's death. The scene he walked into was also completely unanticipated.

Chapter Four

"What the actual fuck?" Gage muttered. Three people, two men and a woman, were in the store. They were line dancing to country music and from the amount of falling around they were doing, they were all well on their way to being drunk. The woman had a half-smoked cigarette in one hand, a wineglass in the other, the red liquid slopping over the rim to land on the cream carpet. Both men held beer bottles and one of them was singing, badly. Various expensive-looking antiques around them had ring marks on their surfaces and a selection of empty bottles littered the floor and the furniture.

"Look, Marla, we have a customer." The man who spoke giggled uncontrollably before collapsing to the floor, where he sat swigging his beer. "Hey man, you wanna drink?" He waved his bottle at Gage.

The woman, Marla, dressed in a white pantsuit and scarlet blouse, sashayed across to Gage. "Well, hey there, handsome, what can I do for you today?" Her suggestive tone and undisguised leer implied that her interest lay somewhere other than selling Gage antiques. Gage put her in her mid-forties. Her makeup was subtle, her hair swept up into some kind of roll, a few wisps escaping. Her blouse had at least two buttons too many undone, revealing the edge of a lacy bra and ample cleavage. Through a haze of cigarette smoke, Gage caught the scent of expensive perfume.

The man on the floor was several years younger, wearing a dark suit and a bow tie that matched Marla's blouse. At some point, he had kicked off his shoes, exposing a pair of red and black striped socks.

"Perhaps you could turn the music down?" When nobody moved, Gage did it himself, turning off the sound system he found concealed beneath the sales desk. "I'm Detective Gage Roskam. I'm here to ask a few questions about the death of Mr. Penton."

The second man, who was much younger than his two colleagues, whooped. "Ding dong, the witch is dead, the wicked witch is dead." He sang with a lot more enthusiasm than talent.

Oh my God. Gage longed for a packet of Tylenol. *If this racket keeps up, I might take them up on their offer of a drink.* "Can I assume you all work here?"

The guy who was still standing grinned and to Gage's huge relief, stopped singing. He was a cute redhead, his face covered in freckles. His hazel eyes were still clear, and Gage guessed he might not be quite as drunk as he was making out.

"I'm Sorrell Sweeting," the redhead said, holding out the hand that wasn't clutching a bottle. "Junior sales assistant at this fine establishment. The lovely lady over there is Marla Deichmann, assistant manager, and my colleague examining the carpet, he's Chet Oram. He's the senior sales guy."

"And is all this" — Gage waved a hand around — "the three of you celebrating your boss's demise?"

"That is *great* detective work," Sorrell admitted with apparent awe and not a trace of sarcasm. "Marla's right, you *are* kinda hot, you wanna dance with me instead? I could see you in a Stetson and a nice tight pair of Wranglers."

Gage took a few rapid steps backward. "No, I do not. Why don't we close up the store then you can show me your break room. Do you have stuff to make coffee?"

"Sure we do," Sorrell said, "one of my very important jobs is to make sure the pot is always full in case a customer wants a cup. The customer is always right, did you know that? They're not really but we have to let them think they are. Did you want to buy something?"

"As I said, I'm a detective investigating Mr. Penton's death." Gage gave up. He went and slipped the latch on the front door himself, turning the 'open' sign to 'closed'. Leaving the three staff to their private party, he explored the store until he found a door that opened onto a staircase. He turned around to find Sorrell right behind him.

"What's up here?"

"Come see." Sorrell pushed past him then ran up the stairs. Gage followed at a more sedate pace, hoping Sorrell didn't fall on his ass. "Poison Penton has his office up here through that door." Sorrell gestured to one side of the room they had entered. "The kitchen's over there, there's a bathroom up those steps and this palatial facility is the staff break room." There were two couches and a low table sharing the space with a dining table and four chairs. Most of the furniture looked like it could have come from a thrift store and certainly didn't reflect the stock in the showroom below.

"Are you steady enough to sort out some coffee for you and your colleagues?" Gage asked.

Sorrell nodded. "Sure, my capacity for hard liquor is a lot better honed than theirs."

"In that case, I'll take a mug too. Creamer, two sugars." Gage squeezed his eyes shut for a moment. "I'm going to go wrangle the others up here."

"Good luck with that."

Gage left Sorrell with the coffeemaker and returned to the sales floor where he found Marla and Chet with their arms around each other's shoulders, attempting the cancan. It wasn't going well, and Gage didn't have too hard a job coaxing them to leave their drinks so they could head upstairs with him.

Sorrell had coffee ready and with a bit of cajoling, Gage got all three of them seated around the table.

"Keep drinking coffee." Gage took a long swallow of his drink, surprised to discover that it was good. "Perhaps we could start by one of you explaining why your boss' death is something to celebrate?" Gage wasn't convinced he was going to get much use out of any of Penton's staff. Marla's eyes were drooping, Chet had a stupid grin on his face, only Sorrell seemed to be anywhere close to sober. "Anyone?"

"It's not a crime to have a few drinks in someone's memory," Sorrell said.

"But that's not what you all were doing, was it?" Gage fixed Sorrell with a gimlet stare. "Don't mess with me. My head hurts, it's already been a long-assed day, and I don't have the time or inclination to listen to your bullshit."

"Ooh, I like it when you get forceful." Sorrell beamed.

"Sorrell... Stop talking or I might feel the need to shoot you, or worse, take you into the precinct, and believe me, the coffee they provide in the interrogation rooms is the color of dirt and tastes about the same."

Sorrell shuddered. "Fine. I wouldn't look good in an orange jumpsuit anyway, not with this hair." He gestured to his ginger mop.

"This is Seattle, not Guantanamo." Chet managed to string a whole sentence together.

"Penton was an unmitigated bastard," Sorrell said. "He was a nasty boss and a thoroughly unpleasant person, the kind who would ignore a starving kitten in the gutter."

"So why didn't you all leave?" Gage looked at each of them in turn.

"The job market in the antiques trade isn't exactly booming," Sorrell said. "Marla has three kids and a waste-of-space husband who walked out on her. I have student debt up to my eyeballs. Chet is paying off his car. It's easy to say if you don't like it then walk, but not all of us have those choices. The rates of pay here aren't bad, the benefits are reasonable... You can put up with a lot for that."

"But won't you all be out of a job now anyway?"

"Hopefully not. Penton's mother jointly owns this place, and she's a sweet lady. She's on her way from Florida and told us to not worry about a thing." He wrapped his hands around his mug, staring into its depths. "You need to understand, Detective, Penton was a nasty piece of work. I'm not saying he deserved what he got, but it's not that surprising. The way he did business earned him a lot of enemies. He was ruthless and mean. He once docked Marla a whole day's pay when she was five minutes late because one of her kids had been puking up his guts all night. Chet is a great salesman even though he's not been here that long, he really likes to get to know his customers and he spent weeks researching some pieces that one particular guy had expressed an interest in. Penton stole the sale from under him, so he lost a big commission."

"What about you, Sorrell?"

"Me? He tried to sell me to some client from Dubai."

"What the fuck? Are you kidding me?"

"There's nothing that would stand up in court, of course." Sorrell's face was flushed. "This guy bought an English dining set that had come out of some stately home. He offered to pay an additional percentage if I accompanied the delivery then stayed as his guest overnight. Penton agreed and made it very clear that I was to do anything the client wanted."

"You didn't…"

"The delivery date isn't until next month. Needless to say I'll be arranging to use the biggest, ugliest, straightest delivery guys we have on the books."

"I thought I had a tough boss… You realize of course that you've just admitted to all three of you having motives to kill Penton."

"Hey, it might not have been appropriate to celebrate quite so blatantly, but none of us actually did the deed. I'd hardly have told you all that if we had. When your colleague, Detective Hernandez, called to tell us the news, she said that you believed he'd been killed some time during the night. We've talked about it. Chet stayed over with a lady friend, Marla was home with the kids and would never leave them alone. Me, I was home by myself. I don't have an alibi, though I was chatting to some buddies on a Dungeons & Dragons forum until around two in the morning. I guess you could check that out."

"Dungeons & Dragons?"

"Role-playing game." Gage squinted at him. "Hey, don't judge. It's fun, keeps me out of trouble, and I have a thing for intelligent guys with glasses. Not that I'm saying the two things are related, but they kind of are. Anyway, a bunch of friends and me — we call ourselves the Gaymers, that's g-a-y-mers. We're a bunch of night owls and spend a lot of time online in the forums. You can check my computer if you like but you have to promise to ignore my search history. I'm a healthy, young gay male and I have interests. Also ignore the dirty laundry on the floor of my bedroom and my roommate, who is way too straight for his own good."

"You would get on far too well with my boyfriend," Gage muttered. "I'm making a note to keep the two of you far apart."

"I knew it! My gaydar is impeccable." Sorrell preened. "I didn't kill Penton, honest."

"Sadly, that's not quite enough for police procedure. Write down the details of this forum." Gage pushed his pad across the table to Sorrell. "I'll need details of your lady friend, Chet, and anyone Marla spoke to that night other than her kids. Now, are any of you aware of anyone else who had a grudge against Mr. Penton or who might have reason to kill him?"

Marla, Chet and Sorrell all laughed. "We'll need more than that notebook if you want us to list all those people," Sorrell said. "Antagonism was Penton's middle name. The only people he sucked up to were the customers with the fattest pocket books. He was only ever interested in what people could do for him, not vice versa."

Marla chugged down her coffee. "Penton's mom and pop ran this place before him and were lovely. I've no idea how he turned out the way he did. He sure fooled them. Unfortunately, they understood their antiques and passed their knowledge onto him. He knew his stuff and had the connections to source high-quality pieces and that kept the customers coming back." She hiccupped and Gage got a blast of alcohol-laced breath in his face.

"It would be helpful if you could give me some names. I'll leave you my details so you can email a list through with any supporting information you can come up with. I suggest you wait until you've all sobered up."

"You're not going to arrest us, then?" Sorrell asked, sounding wistful. "I can appreciate a shiny pair of handcuffs."

"I'll just bet you can," Chet muttered.

Sorrell winked at him. "What else can we do for you, Detective Roskam?"

Gage tapped his pen on the table. "Has anything out of the ordinary happened in the store recently? Have you seen any customers that perhaps didn't fit? Did you witness any arguments or have any other problems?"

"A few days ago, some bum got in here. He reeked of booze and was shouting about wanting pie," Sorrell explained. "He almost knocked over a valuable vase, but I managed to catch it."

"It was like Sorrell said," Chet butted in. "The guy was drunker than I am now. It took forever to get him out of the store. Penton wasn't here that day. He was over at the warehouse."

"Warehouse?" Gage gave Chet a questioning glance.

"It's a storage facility down by the river." Sorrell said. "It's where Penton kept stock when it arrived from overseas. You want the address?" He reached for the pad before Gage could agree and scribbled a few lines.

"I'll check it out. I think that's it for now." Gage handed each of the salespeople a card. "Here's where you can reach me if you think of anything useful." He pushed his chair back then got to his feet. "Don't be planning any trips out of the area. I may need to talk to you all again. If someone could call me when Mrs. Penton arrives, that would be helpful."

"I'll do that," Sorrell offered. "Let me show you out."

Sorrell accompanied Gage as far as the sidewalk. "Is there a drugstore anywhere close?" Gage asked.

"One block down on the other side of the street. Have we given you a headache?"

"It's been building all day. I'll leave my Jeep in your lot and walk over there," Gage said. "Don't call the cops to report an abandoned vehicle, okay?"

Sorrell chuckled. "No promises."

Gage rolled his eyes. "Go sober up or you'll be the one needing Tylenol." He gave Sorrell a wave then strolled off in the direction of the drugstore.

Having bought a bottle of water and some painkillers, Gage administered self-care after returning to his Jeep. He drove toward the river, heading for Penton's storage facility.

A combination of Seattle traffic, a long diversion around a work zone and a missed turn meant it took

Gage over an hour to find the warehouse. The parking lot was opposite the building, which was surrounded by a high wall. Gage pulled in, turned off the engine and leaned back in his seat with a sigh. He missed Sancha's company. They kept each other motivated, and she always knew when Gage was in a bit of a slump. He cracked open his bottle of water for another drink, debating whether to swallow more tablets. He decided an overdose was not the way to go even though the pills he'd already taken weren't having much effect.

He kept an eye on the storage facility across the street. It wasn't inviting. It hadn't been modernized like so many of the properties along Seattle's lengthy waterfront. This place was red brick, two stories and the wall around it bristled with coils of razor wire. It could have passed as a prison or an insane asylum in a 1930s movie. Gage retrieved his gun from the glove compartment then slipped it into his shoulder holster. He was about to go in but decided to give Landry a quick call. "Hey, sweetheart, are you behaving yourself?"

"Of course I am!" Landry's indignant tone made Gage laugh. "But what about you? I got a message from Sancha about her having to go away. Are you all alone?"

"I am. I'm flying solo until I pick up some Brit from the airport tonight. I have to drop him at his hotel so I'll be late, though it shouldn't be as bad as last night. His flight gets in at seven."

"Where are you? What are you doing now?"

"Legwork. I paid a visit to Penton's Antiquarium and I'm about to take a look at his storage facility though I'm not sure how far I'll get without a warrant. I'm sitting in the parking lot at the moment."

"Don't forget to eat. With no Sancha to take care of you, you'll forget. I know you."

"I'll pick up a hot dog when I'm done here." Gage visualized Landry shaking his head, lips pursed.

"In that case I'll make sure we have something healthy tonight. Be warned, there will be green stuff involved."

"Should I ask how many trips you and Petey have made to the café for baked goods so far today?"

"No, you shouldn't. Oh, customers, I have to go." Landry disconnected.

"Brat," Gage muttered under his breath. "Tonight, I'm going to make sure my hand has plenty of time to connect with that boy's backside." He took a few minutes to check in at the precinct, letting one of the other detectives know where he was. There were no messages, so he locked the Jeep then strolled across the street to the warehouse gate. He had to use an intercom and hold his ID up to a camera before he was granted entrance. There was a distinct chill in the air and a light drizzle had started. Gage picked up his pace and made a beeline for a side door labeled with a small sign that said 'Reception'. The building might not be inviting but at least inside it would be dry.

Chapter Five

There was another camera above the reception door and Gage held his ID up again, tapping his foot until the door clicked open. Everything about the room he entered was grimy. The floor in front of the counter was bare concrete, dried up gum and cigarette butts created a pattern of neglect. A tattered poster advertising Coney Island decorated one wall—one corner of it smudged by a dubious rust-colored stain. The man behind the counter was as grubby as his workspace. A greasy comb-over topped a bloated head and his skin was dotted with pimples. He had muddy brown eyes and a scar bisected one brow. His sweater should have been plain but was splattered with a variety of stains. Gage repressed a shudder.

"What can I do for ya?"

Gage couldn't quite place the accent. If he'd had to guess, he would have said New York, maybe Queens. "Your name?"

"Abner Gore, at your service. Are you looking to rent a space?"

"I'm interested in someone who's already one of your customers, Arthur Penton."

Gore nodded his head far too much. "Could be, could be... Confidentiality is the watchword here though, you understand."

"This is an active homicide investigation," Gage said. "I don't have time for this crap. I *know* Penton is a customer."

"Well, aren't you a live one? He's dead I guess?"

"I didn't say that."

"Stands to reason. The man was obnoxious. Sooner or later he was going to get what was coming to him."

Gage didn't confirm or deny Gore's assumption. "What can you tell me about his account?"

"Not a lot without a warrant. He has one of our biggest spaces. Ground floor, access for a van. Account was automated, never got behind with the payments."

"Any trouble around here recently?"

"The usual. Kids trying to get over the fence. A couple security lights taken out because they tossed rocks at them. A few nonpayers that get overexcited when we sell off their units. You'd be amazed how many people conveniently forget they have stuff in storage until they get past the third payment reminder and show up on auction day."

"You have decent security in here." Gage spotted several devices and the computer Gore sat in front of was high-end. "I'm guessing this place isn't quite what it seems."

"Appearances can be deceptive and that suits a lot of our clients. Professional thieves are more likely to target buildings that look like they might have stuff inside worth stealing."

Gage couldn't imagine Penton storing high-value antiques somewhere without security systems. "I guess so."

"You wanna take a look around?" Gore asked. "I can't let you into Penton's unit without a warrant, but there ain't no harm in you taking a stroll around the building to get the lay of the land as it were."

"I'll do that."

"Make a note of how cooperative I'm being." Gore's grin exposed a set of yellowing teeth. He heaved himself off his stool, circled the counter then punched a code into a keypad next to a side door. "Have yourself a blast. I gotta stay here to watch the cameras." Gage nodded. He didn't want Gore any closer to him than necessary. "This building is joined to a second one behind it. There's a covered walkway between the two. Penton has the back left corner of the second building. Ground floor. Number twelve."

The door slammed behind Gage leaving him in an austere gray corridor. As he moved, automated lights flickered on, illuminating a few feet. They went off again behind him. When he looked back, the passageway was totally dark. On either side, a series of black steel doors had numbers painted on them. Gage moved quickly, noting cameras placed at regular intervals. It was lighter in the connecting corridor but much colder in the second building, and Gage wished he had worn a heavier coat. He passed the foot of some stairs and glanced up into the darkness. There didn't seem much point in exploring the second story before he got to Penton's unit. He had passed door eleven when he thought he heard a scratching noise. "There'd better not be any fucking rats in here," he muttered. "I hate rats." Landry had told him once that he was never more than six feet away from a rat. He had given Landry a sound spanking for that useless piece of information, which now took up way too much space in Gage's head. A glint of light caught his eye, and he spotted a cigarette butt on the floor that was still glowing. *Should have asked Gore if there was anyone else back here.*

He approached the door to unit twelve with some caution, reaching inside his jacket to release the snap on his holster, though he didn't draw his gun. Being isolated in a small pool of light was making his skin crawl. Number twelve's door was open, just a crack. Gage listened hard but couldn't hear anything inside. He drew his gun then pushed the door. A high-pitched squeal from the hinges made Gage curse. If there *was* anyone in there, they knew he was coming. All he could see were the dim shapes of pieces of furniture. A whisper of breeze against his face alerted him to movement. He whirled around straight into a blow to the side of his head. He went down hard, vision blurring.

"Fuck!" He rolled onto his back, trying to raise his gun as the dim shape of a man loomed over him. His arm shook uncontrollably, and it proved impossible to pull the trigger before everything went black.

* * * *

"Have you seen the Antiquarium's website?" Petey asked, staring at the computer screen. "The value of their stock must be astronomical. There's not much here that I'd want in my place, though some bits are really pretty."

"Mr. Lao and I were having a look yesterday, doing a bit of poking around to see what we could find out," Landry said. "Some of those things seem to be awful dust traps. None of it would fit in here and our customers wouldn't want that kind of stuff anyway. It all seems a bit fancy for me. It's stuff you wouldn't actually want to use. I'd be afraid to put a coffee cup down anywhere."

"And that's a big problem for you," Petey crowed.

"Just being practical."

"Penton has a newsletter sign-up and a backlist of archived editions. Do you think it would be worth downloading them and having a read?"

"I didn't spot that. Definitely." Landry shivered, a sudden wave of cold passing over him. "Can you feel a draft coming from somewhere?"

"No." Petey gave him a curious look. "In fact, I was just thinking it was really warm in here today."

Landry reached for his phone, a niggling kernel of doubt settling in the pit of his stomach. He texted Gage, just a simple message asking Gage to call him back. He always started with a text when he wanted to get in touch, in case Gage was in a situation where his cell ringing could put him in danger if he'd forgotten to put it on silent. He texted back as soon as he could even if it was only to send an emoji, knowing Landry needed reassurance.

"What's up?" Petey asked.

"Just a weird feeling that something's wrong," Landry replied. "It's probably nothing. I guess I'm still a bit jumpy after finding the body."

"You should listen to your gut, you've been right more often than not."

"What's the saying that Mr. Lao uses? It's as if an ancestor walked over his grave, which is uber creepy by the way, but kind of fits. Why isn't Gage calling me back? I wish Sancha hadn't had to go away. He's on his own today and I don't like that. No backup is a terrible plan."

"You're babbling. Why don't you call the precinct and talk to one of his colleagues? They might be able to give you some information. Seriously, call them, Landry. Don't ignore it."

Landry nodded. "I'm going to feel like an idiot if there's nothing wrong and I'm going to blame you, you know that, don't you?"

"Of course, but if I was saying this about Carson, you'd be pushing me to call the firehouse."

Landry called the precinct and asked for Gage's boss. To his surprise, he was put through straight away.

"Landry, my favorite person. What can I do for you?"

Landry loved that Gage's boss always came straight to the point without any hesitation. "You're going to think I'm a complete idiot, but I've got a bad feeling. I texted Gage and he didn't reply. It's only been a few minutes but... Ignore me, I'm being paranoid."

"Let me look into it. I'll track him down and give him a good chewing out for worrying you. As far as I know, he's not doing anything where he would be out of contact but he could be in a blind spot or something. Try not to worry."

"Thanks for listening."

"Anytime, I've been around the block enough times to know better than to ignore gut feeling."

Landry disconnected, a little less anxious knowing that Gage's boss would do what he promised. There wasn't anything else Landry could do to help so he joined Petey at the computer. "Try searching under 'news', let's see if Penton ever got his face in the papers."

Petey did a bit of rapid searching. "He definitely liked a night out, didn't he?"

Landry nodded, looking at pages of pictures. "Most of this coverage is local stuff, isn't it? Business-related dinners, charity bashes, that kind of thing. Go back a bit further."

After scanning through a few more articles, Petey stabbed at the screen. "This is more interesting. This is in a British newspaper. It's an article about a big auction at a place called Crowberry Castle."

Landry peered over Petey's shoulder. "Well, you're right, this is much more interesting. So the castle's contents were auctioned after the owner died suddenly and the widow couldn't pay the death duties—I guess that's what they call inheritance taxes. If we can find the auction house that handled the sale, there might be a catalog we can look at. Is Penton mentioned in the article?"

"International antiques dealers from around the world were present for the sale, including Arthur Penton from the United States... Then it lists a few others from France, South Africa, Japan... This must have been a big deal."

"I think if we're going to get into some heavy research here, we need refreshments," Landry said. "I'll run next door for drinks. What would you like?"

"I could use a Sprite," Petey said. "This is thirsty work."

"Okay, I won't be long."

Landry made a dash for the café and whooped when he found there was no line. Mary rolled her eyes at him. "Only you would be happy that I have no business," she said.

"I'm your best and most favorite customer," Landry said. "And besides, there was a line out the door earlier, so don't try that sob story on me."

Mary huffed. "You want your usual?"

Landry nodded. "And a cold Sprite for Petey, please. How's your love life?"

"None of your business." Mary tackled the coffee machine and soon the hiss of steam and the aroma of freshly ground beans wafted in Landry's direction.

"Oh, come on. It's because of me that you met the big hunk."

"Landry, I'd prefer not to be reminded that I met the man because of the dead body in your doorway, thank you kindly."

"Hey, it's a good story for your grandkids."

"We just met! Don't start planning the wedding yet."

Landry shrugged. "I need plenty of notice to plan my new outfit, just saying."

"I'll bet that detective of yours looks great in a tux," Mary said, handing Landry his coffee across the counter.

"He looks even better out of one," Landry said, grinning.

"Now, there's food for thought. Speaking of, you want any goodies?"

"I'll take a bag of donut holes, please. Petey and I can share them, and it's like charitable eating, isn't it, because they're a waste product?"

"I love your attempt at justifying your sugar habit."

"You ever wonder why they get called holes? I mean the hole is what's left, empty space, not the yummy bit. I think they should be called plugs because if you put them back in, they'd be plugging the holes."

"You have the most peculiar mind, Landry Carran. Some might say you're fixated on plugs and holes. Can't imagine why. Now get back to work."

"That did sound bad, didn't it?"

"Gage has his hands full with you, doesn't he?"

"Don't you think that's kind of a personal question?" Landry got ready to run.

"Out! You wait till I talk to Gage!"

Cackling, Landry slammed money on the counter, gathered up his purchases then scooted back to the safety of Treasure Trove where Petey was ringing up a customer, chattering away like he and the pink-haired lady had been friends for life. Landry waited until he was done, and the smiling customer had left, before dumping his goodies on the counter.

"What did we sell?"

"That beautiful Norwegian silver and enamel jewelry set. The woman wanted it as an anniversary gift for her wife. Would you believe they've been together for fifty years?"

"Wow. I wonder if me and Gage will make it that far, or you and Carson."

"We will," Petey said, full of certainty. "No one else would put up with you. Of course, I might have to make Carson wear a paper bag over his head because he's so hot everyone wants to steal him." Petey thrust his hand into the bag of donut holes. "Ooh, yum."

"I'm going to need a while to process the various parts of that statement." Landry took a long swig of coffee. "I can't believe I bought you treats. Gimme that bag."

Between them, they demolished the entire bag of sugary goodness and after dealing with another two customers, settled back behind the computer. This time Landry took charge of the keyboard. It didn't take him that long to find more information about the country house debt sale.

"Okay, so the auction took place on site at the house, actually the castle, over two days and there were over eight hundred lots. Wow, most of the coverage is about the pieces that got the highest prices — a pair of punch bowls, which sold for thirty-two thousand pounds and, holy cow, a rare Chinese vase, which went for over three hundred thousand. The sale in total made almost four million and every item sold. What's that in dollars?"

"Mega bucks!"

"Let's see if there's a full list of the lots. Penton would have been interested in the furniture, not porcelain or glass." After a bit more tapping, Landry found some more information. "Okay, here we go. It says here that the sale included English and French furniture, Chinese porcelain, silver, wine, books and paintings.

"There was furniture by Chippendale, John Henri Riesener, Andre Charles Boulle — every famous cabinetmaker you can imagine. It must have been an amazing occasion, though kinda sad for the owners of the castle." Landry downloaded the catalog so that he could take a closer look later.

"Is there anything more about how the owner died?" Petey asked.

There were a few links to news articles from the auction coverage, and Landry found an obituary in The

Times. "The owner of the castle was the Right Honorable Cecil Winterton. He was only fifty-six."

"That's not old," Petey said. "Does it say what he died of?"

"No…wait, there's a little bit here about an inquest. His death was sudden and unexpected. Heart attack. There's a picture."

"Bit of a silver fox," Petey said, examining the photograph.

"You're not wrong. It doesn't say anything about the death being suspicious. His daughter inherited but the death duties were crippling—not much of a motive to off dear old pop."

"Then perhaps we're heading down a blind alley."

"Hmm, could be. Penton surely bought stock from all over the place, but Gage mentioned he was picking up some Brit from the airport who was going to be assisting with the investigation. There's a UK link here somewhere and this seems likely."

"Well then, we should wait for Gage to meet this guy and let slip a few more juicy details."

Landry laughed. "Gage doesn't let anything slip. I'll have to interrogate him."

"Sounds delicious."

"Doesn't it though." Landry's cell ringing interrupted his daydreams. "Oh my God, do you think he was listening?" He answered the call. "Oh, hey, Bald…I mean Captain Henry. Any news?"

"I know what they call me, Landry. Are you alone?"

"No…why?" Landry's hand started to shake.

"Don't panic. He's okay."

"Why shouldn't he be?" Landry squeaked. Petey guided him to a chair.

"We tracked him down to a storage place by the river. Someone jumped him."

"They what? Is he hurt? Do I need to get to the hospital? Which one…oh, I don't know what to do."

"He's fine. He'll likely have a headache for a few days, but the paramedics checked him out at the scene. Stubborn S.O.B. refused a trip to the ER."

"Where is he?"

"Heading back here to the precinct. His cell got stomped on, but he'll call you as soon as he gets here."

"Why isn't that mule-headed idiot coming home?"

"Because he's mule-headed."

"Can you not yell at him or something? Send him home?"

"Landry…how far do you think that would get me?"

"Good point. If he doesn't call me the instant he sets foot in the precinct, tell him he's in a whole bucket-load of trouble, okay?"

"I'll tell him. Cora-Beth would like the two of you over for dinner real soon."

"Tell Cora-Beth it would be our pleasure…if Gage survives. You'd overlook a little justifiable homicide, wouldn't you?"

Captain Henry chuckled. "I'll let her know to get in touch and arrange a date."

Once the call had ended, Landry slumped in his seat. "Petey, if that man of mine gets himself dead, I'm gonna kill him."

"That sounds like a triple espresso statement. I'll be right back."

"Petey!" Landry called after him as he scuttled toward the door. "Bring all the sugar. A giant bear claw for clawing my bear."

"You got it!"

"Jesus, Gage, way to give your boyfriend heart failure," Landry muttered, eyeing his cell, willing it to ring. "I think it's about time I tied *you* to the bed."

Chapter Six

"Fuck me. I always knew when the day came, I'd be on the down elevator." Gage closed the eye he'd just opened.

"You're not dead, Gage, and despite the unsavory nature of this place, it isn't hell. I'd imagine that's going to be warmer."

"Then what the ever-loving fuck are you doing here?" Gage had to open his eyes again. "I'm either having a bad dream or some kind of hallucination. James fucking Ellery cannot be here." He dragged himself from his prone position to sit with his back against the wall. He didn't think an attempt to stand was wise.

"A few points if I may. One, my middle name is Piers, not fucking. Two, my presence here has let you off a trip to the airport and three, I just saved your sorry behind, so a little gratitude would be appreciated."

"Fuck off."

"Feeling a bit cranky, are we?"

"Cranky doesn't even begin to describe my current mood."

Ellery crouched in front of Gage. There was a gun dangling from his finger. "Yours, I believe?"

"And this dumpster fire of a day keeps on improving." Gage took the gun. "Where did you get this?"

"You dropped it when you walked into ski mask guy's fist. You should perhaps consider not doing that in the future. It looked painful."

Before Gage could ask one of the several hundred questions buzzing around his head, two uniformed cops, guns extended, charged down the passageway.

"Hands in the air! Detective Roskam, are you okay?"

Ellery raised his hands, smug grin on his face.

"I'm good and I can't believe I'm saying this, but the smarmy Brit is with us." Both cops seemed disappointed. "Yeah, I know. I'd quite like to shoot him too."

"The captain sent us over here. Something about a hunch that you were getting yourself into trouble."

"Whose hunch?"

"Who do you think?"

"Landry." Gage sighed.

"He makes the best cookies." The cop smirked. "You should keep him."

"You keep your goddamn hands off my boy's cookies," Gage spluttered.

Ellery grinned. "You might want to call in the medical chaps. He got clocked over the head, and though I know he has an exceptionally hard skull, a precautionary examination might be in order."

"What the fuck is he talking about?" Both cops looked confused.

"He thinks I might need a meat wagon."

"Well, why the fuck didn't he say so?" One cop got on his radio while the other peered into the storage unit before making his way cautiously inside.

"Two nations divided by a common language," Ellery muttered. He held out a hand. "Want to get off the floor or does your backside enjoy cold concrete? I'm not one to kink shame."

"I hate you so much right now." Gage took the offered hand and Ellery hauled him upright. For a moment, the walls slipped out of focus, but Ellery kept Gage from falling. "I want to know what the hell you're doing here?"

"There's no one else here now." The cop who'd been poking around in the storage unit returned to the corridor. "Let's take this outside."

"This whole area needs to be taped off," Gage said, trying to concentrate. "The passage and the unit. Get forensics in here."

The cop rolled his eyes. "No shit, Detective."

"I think the nice policeman objects to you telling him how to do his job," Ellery said. "He seems perfectly capable, so how about we go get some fresh air where we can see if there are any dents in that thick skull of yours."

Gage growled. "I really want to hit something. Someone. Anything." He stomped along the passage back to the front office. "I want to talk to that idiot manning the desk, who didn't mention that he'd let someone else back there."

They found Abner Gore cowering behind his terminal. As soon as they came through the door, he held up his hands. "Not my fault!"

Gage took a deep breath, counted to ten and schooled his features into a semblance of calm. "Tell me you got what happened on tape."

Gore nodded. "I saw what went down and called the cops, but they were already on the way."

"And the guy that attacked me?"

"Barreled back through here at a run. He wasn't hanging around."

"Did you get a good look at him?"

"He was wearing a ski mask. He'll be on the footage too but there won't be much to see."

"Was he wearing a ski mask when he came in?" Sarcasm laced Gage's tone. Next to him, Ellery snickered.

"Assuming it's the same guy, he had a scarf over the bottom half of his face and a big hood up on his coat. He may as well have been wearing a ski mask. It's a cold day, for fuck's sake."

"It's Seattle, not Anchorage. Did he have an accent? Did you notice anything unusual about him? Other than the violent tendencies."

"Do you know how many people I see every day in this job? I don't make notes about everyone who comes in. If they have a code, they go right through."

"So he had a rental unit? He must have if he had a code, right?"

"I guess so, or he could have a code from someone else."

"So there's no requirement for people to sign in? Isn't that against fire regulations?"

"I keep a tally so I know how many people are in the building. I've no idea whether that's against regulations or not, I do what I'm told by the boss. Some people come in and out several times a day. They don't want to be held up by me. Bad for business."

"We'll need all your security footage. How long do you keep it for?"

"It overwrites every week on a Sunday night."

Gage rubbed the back of his neck. "Great. Fucking great."

"Hey, you can put him back on the rack later. Time you saw the paramedics." Ellery gave Gage a firm shove in the direction of the door.

An ambulance was waiting, and Gage submitted to the ministrations of a young woman with fluorescent green hair who insisted on shining a light into his eyes, which seemed counterintuitive to reducing the pain in his head. He confessed to the throbbing. To her credit, the paramedic only made one attempt to convince Gage a hospital visit was required.

"Unless there's a hole in my skull, I'm not going near any hospital. Am I done?" Gage asked, his impatience a symptom of his headache rather than annoyance.

"Sure. Try not to get bashed over the head again today." The paramedic grinned. "The two remaining brain cells might not survive."

"I'll do my best."

"Who's your friend? He attached?" Gage looked around for Ellery who was hovering nearby. Despite having just been involved in a skirmish, his appearance was immaculate. He wore all black, which made his light blond hair and blue eyes stand out even more than usual. "He's pretty but he has psychological issues, steer clear."

The paramedic shrugged. "Worth a shot."

"Stop lounging around like you're waiting for a call on a modeling shoot," Gage grumbled to Ellery. "I need to eat. I'm already gonna be in enough trouble with Landry. I do not need to add missing meals to my catalog of misdemeanors."

"That boy has you right where he wants you, doesn't he?" Ellery smirked. "What's it to be? Don't say hot dog because I refuse to consume an unidentifiable meat product."

"Do not diss wholesome American food. Do you have transport?"

"I took a cab. I was surprised to learn that taxi drivers here are just as educational as those in New York. Were you aware that there is a British pub on North 36th Street called the George and Dragon, which serves fish and chips, bangers and mash and a full English breakfast? My driver was a regular."

"Consider me enlightened. I'm tempted to force a hot dog down your irritating throat, but my head tells me I need to sit down. You can slum it in my Jeep and we'll go find a diner, where you're going to give me an explanation of why you are here using a false name and what the ever-loving fuck you were doing at that storage facility at the exact same time I was getting jumped."

"My pleasure. Do you need to call that delicious little sample of yours?"

Gage cursed under his breath. "I'd better if I want to keep breathing." He patted his pockets but there was no sign of his cell.

"Are you looking for this?" Ellery handed over the phone, complete with smashed screen and cracked case.

"Well, fuck." Gage gestured to one of the cops stringing up the crime scene tape around the front door of the building. "Have you relayed information back to the precinct?"

"Sure, the captain wanted to know how many pieces you were in. He wants you back at base."

"Great." Gage turned back to Ellery. "You didn't hear that bit about the precinct and neither did I. My boss will call Landry. Once we've eaten, we'll run by the store to reassure him. *You* will stay in the Jeep."

Ellery shrugged. "He's going to find out I'm here sooner or later."

"And I need to pick the right moment to tell him, or I'll have blue balls for months."

"You can use my mobile to call him." Ellery held out a top of the range iPhone. "Don't make him wait. It's your voice he needs to hear, not your boss'."

"I want it noted for the record that I hate it when you're right." Gage made the call.

"Landry, it's me."

"Gage! Whose cell are you using? This isn't your number. Where are you? Are you all right? Your captain called me, and he said you refused to go to the ER. Why would you do that? You are one dumb, stubborn…"

"Slow down, Lan! I'm fine. I was knocked out briefly but you know me, hard head. I'm going for something to eat then I'll cruise by the store as soon as I can."

"Should you be driving? I should come down there and beat you so hard. What were you thinking, going somewhere without backup? Your captain should ground you. We have an invite to dinner by the way."

Gage held the cell away from his ear and scowled at Ellery, who doubled over laughing. "I went to a storage facility, not some biker gang drug den. There was no reason to think I'd be in any danger."

"There are biker gang drug dens in Seattle?" Landry's voice got higher and louder. "Oh God."

"It was an example, Landry, that's all."

"A bad one!"

"Calm down, sweetheart. Everything's fine."

"Did you just tell me to calm down?"

"No! I wouldn't dare. Is Petey there with you?"

"He's here. Where else would he be? I'm stuck here in the store while you're out getting yourself beaten up!" Landry ended the sentence with a strangled sob.

"Get Petey to make you some herbal tea. I will be there soon, after I've ironed out a few issues."

"Herbal...you hate me, don't you?"

"I love you and tonight I will give you a demonstration of just how much, but for now, I have to work, and you have to stop tying your tail in knots. That's an order, Landry."

"Yes, Sir." Gage visualized Landry's lip jutting in an enormous pout and smiled. "Don't have a tail."

"That could be remedied."

"You...I...no puppy play, Sir!"

"I'm thinking about a nice, fat butt plug with a waggy rubber tail."

"Going back to work now."

"Good plan." Gage disconnected then handed the cell back to Ellery, who didn't say a word.

"Stop smirking." Gage marched over to his Jeep.

"I'd forgotten how much entertainment value I got out of you two."

"Why aren't you in fucking jail?"

"Charm and talent."

"Fucked if I can see much of either."

"Honestly, Gage, your language is a disgrace. You need a wider selection of expletives."

"I'll do my level best to fucking surprise you. I'm sure you'll give me ample fucking opportunity."

"No doubt. Feed me, Detective."

Gage drove a few blocks to a waterside diner he knew was popular with the local beat cops. He'd only had coffee there himself but if the local guys liked it, the food was guaranteed to be good, cheap and plentiful. There were also plenty of booths, which meant he could interrogate Ellery in relative privacy.

Once they were situated, a smiling server took their orders and brought coffee and iced waters. Gage swallowed more tablets in the hope that his continuing headache might abate. He didn't have much confidence. Dealing with Ellery was likely to give him hives as well as a full-blown migraine.

He'd promised Landry he'd eat so, though he wasn't sure his stomach could take it, Gage ordered a plain omelet. With unconcealed glee, Ellery asked for sliders with a side of fries and waffles with syrup. Gage sipped his water and fought back the urge to punch the smirk off Ellery's face.

"So, how about you start talking?" Gage made eye contact and held it.

"Food first?"

"Nope. If what you tell me makes sense, I might let you eat."

"How's your head?"

"Getting worse by the second, which does nothing for either my temper or my patience, Ellery."

"Don't you think by now you should be calling me James?"

"When hell freezes over." Ellery dumped two cubes of sugar into his coffee then spent far too long stirring it. "I'm really tempted to shove that spoon where the sun don't shine. Talk."

"So much aggression. Very well, I'll stop teasing you. You're far too easy a target, anyway. Where do you want me to begin?"

"How about we start with current events. You can fill me in on the background later. What's your interest in this case?"

"Okay, the abridged version because I know you have a short attention span. I'm still working as a freelance investigator for big insurance companies. One of them held the life insurance policy for the Right Honorable Cecil Winterton, until recently the owner of Crowberry Castle in Suffolk, England."

"I'm guessing he's dead then?"

"Yes, and he wasn't old. Cause of death was a heart attack and, on the surface, that's a possibility because he'd had a few health issues. However, there were a couple of massive life insurance policies on him running into the millions. My employers do not like those kind of numbers."

"Aren't the proceeds of life insurance policies subject to inheritance tax in the UK?"

"Yes, they are unless they're held in trust, but the beneficiaries of the policies weren't family members."

"Ah. So your bosses are looking for a reason not to pay."

"Got it in one."

"So who does benefit?"

"Winterton's business partners, two of them. Their story is that they all took out policies on each other to protect the business if one of them should die unexpectedly because their investments would form part of their estates and go to their families."

"Sounds plausible."

"It does, but who's to say what either of them would do with the money once it's in their hands. They have no legal duty to reinvest. They could let the company go down the tubes and retire to a beach in the south of France if they felt like it.

"There was an inquest, but it concluded cause of death was a heart attack. I've been asked to conduct an investigation to allay suspicions that all is not right. In my humble opinion, this all stinks like a month-old kipper. Oh, you're a little green — as in relative of Shrek green."

"Stop talking about old kippers."

"My sincerest apologies."

"Fuck off."

"You have such a beautiful turn of phrase."

"Get on with it!" Gage swallowed more water. "Why are you in the US?"

"Certain people are showing too much interest in a shipment of furniture and other antiques that came over here after an estate sale at the castle. It's possible that there is evidence that Winterton's death wasn't natural and that that evidence is concealed somewhere in the shipment."

"What do you mean when you say there's interest?"

"Someone appears to be mopping up loose ends. The manager from the shipping company that handled the export process met with an unfortunate accident."

Gage frowned. "What kind of accident?"

"He drove his car off a flyover. That's overpass to you non-English speakers. Witnesses said it seemed out of control but the resulting fireball meant there wasn't enough of it, or him, left to know if the car had been sabotaged or if the issue was with him."

"Nasty."

"That's not all. There was then a blaze at the shipping company's offices and all the paperwork relating to the container was destroyed. Two clerks were killed in the fire."

"Holy crap, the bodies are piling up."

"Indeed. Someone very ruthless is protecting his or her interests. I'm here because I'm following the cargo."

"So you were already in the storage place when I got there."

"Uh, not quite."

"What do you mean…? Wait. Oh, you sonofabitch. You were following me."

"That bang on the head didn't addle your brain completely then."

"Stop fucking smiling."

"I already knew you were the detective on the case this end, so where better to start than by tracking your sorry tail? Besides, cabbies love it when you say 'follow that car!'"

Gage groaned. "I hate you so much right now."

"You keep saying that, even though I saved your behind. I'll have you know it took some smooth talking to get past that idiot on the reception desk. Thankfully, he can't tell the difference between a Seattle PD badge and the fake one I picked up on eBay."

"Oh my God."

"I gather you weren't expecting to find anyone at the storage place?"

"Because I always walk into dangerous situations without backup. Of course I didn't! I came from the Antiquarium after staff there told me about the storage location. I didn't even have a warrant yet, I was having an initial look around, that's all."

"Could someone from there have beaten you to the warehouse?"

Gage considered it. "I guess it's possible. I stopped at a drugstore then got a bit lost en route so it took a while to get there. I don't think it's likely though. The three staff I interviewed had been partying hard when I found them, and it would be too easy to go back and find out if any of them left after I did. I think this was someone else and it was pure bad luck that I caught them breaking into Penton's unit. I'll check it out though."

Their food arrived and Gage was happy to have a reason not to talk. He grimaced at Ellery's various delighted noises as he inhaled his meal. Gage was much less enthused about his omelet but once he started eating, his stomach rumbled its gratitude. He still had a lot of questions for Ellery, but so far the Brit sounded plausible. *Fuck, I must have brain damage after all if I'm thinking that.* He made eye contact with Ellery who gave him a knowing grin.

"Fuck off," Gage grumbled.

James Ellery kept smiling.

Chapter Seven

In the end, Gage decided that visiting Landry whilst James Ellery was within a hundred yards was excessively dangerous. He dropped Ellery at his hotel, which of course was the height of five-star luxury, before tackling the traffic. Ellery had promised to stay put, confessing to lingering jetlag. Gage took that promise with a pinch of salt. He didn't trust Ellery as far as he could throw him. Still, he had a few hours respite and a bigger problem to tackle.

He approached Treasure Trove with some trepidation. He'd timed his arrival so that it was a couple of hours before closing, which meant if he had to escape, Landry wouldn't be able to run after him without abandoning the store.

"Damn, I forgot about Petey." Chasing was a possibility, after all. *With any luck, the place will be packed with antique foragers.* Gage debated stopping in at the café to buy bribe material but shook his head. "Man up, Roskam. Big bad Dom, remember?" The moment he opened the door there was a yell and Landry hurtled toward him. Gage caught his boyfriend, absorbing the impact of Landry's uncontrolled run.

"Glad to see me, huh?" Petey waved from behind the cash desk. "Hey, Petey."

"Hi, Gage, it was nice knowing you." Petey giggled.

"You big lug, don't you ever scare me like that again." Landry smacked Gage's bicep before hugging him again, even harder. "I am so mad at you. You should never be allowed out without Sancha again, you understand? You wait until she calls. I'm gonna tell her that you have to be confined to desk duty whenever she goes away."

Gage rested his chin on Landry's hair. "I'm fine. It wasn't anything serious."

"I like your head just the way it is, thank you very much. It doesn't need any more dents." Landry was doing his best impression of an octopus, clinging on for dear life.

"You're right. How about I go lie down for an hour or two while you and Petey finish your day? My head *is* a little sore." Gage felt no guilt in playing the sympathy card.

Landry disengaged then took a step back. He laid his fingers against Gage's forehead. "You *are* a bit warm. A nap is a good idea. Take some pain pills, drink some water then pull the drapes. I'll come wake you for some dinner and then you have to tell me everything."

"You know I can't give you details about an ongoing case, baby." Gage took in Landry's narrowed eyes and sighed. "But I'll tell you what I can."

Landry's face lit up with a beaming smile. "And I can tell you what Petey and I have found out too."

"What do you mean? Landry, have you been poking around where you shouldn't?"

"Maybe?"

"We've talked about this. You are not to get involved in this case. I won't have you in danger. We've been there, done that."

"But I haven't got the T-shirt yet. I haven't done anything dangerous, promise."

"We'll talk about this later." *Preferably when you're naked and laid across my lap for a spanking.*

"Yes, Sir."

Oh, he's in full-on brat mode. Lying down in a darkened room is a fine idea. "Be good. Even you should be able to manage that for two hours."

"I have no idea what you mean!" Landry planted a smacking kiss on Gage's cheek. "Seriously, go rest. You look like a big pile of plop."

"I'm guessing that's not good."

"No, Sir."

Getting horizontal had appeal. Gage was reluctant to leave Landry to his own devices, but if he didn't deal with his throbbing head, Landry would run rings around him later. He headed for their apartment and once inside he left the lights off. The dimness was bliss. He grabbed a bottle of water from the kitchen and chugged half of it, then swallowed two pills before making his way to the bedroom. He kicked off his shoes, removed his jacket then lay on the bed, leaving the rest of his clothes on. He put his backup cell on charge, made sure the volume was turned up on the ringer, then closed his eyes. For a while, he dozed in the strange halfway state between awake and asleep. There was too much going on in his head for him to truly relax but in the dark, with his eyes closed, his headache subsided to a dull throb.

When his cell rang, it took him a moment to realize it wasn't a dream. Feeling groggy, Gage groped in the direction of the noise and managed to knock the handset onto the floor.

"Fuck." He knuckled his eyes in an attempt to wake up more fully then leaned over the side of the bed. His cell went to voicemail, but seconds later rang again. It was an older model he'd kept in case anything happened to his new one and he was grateful for the foresight. It had to be someone from work calling because the only people that had the old number on record were his captain and Landry. He hadn't been bothered to transfer the number—he gave it out to so few people. Landry wouldn't be calling when he could run upstairs if he needed to.

Fumbling with the old buttons, Gage finally managed to answer. "Roskam. This had better be good."

"Surprise. Did I wake you?"

"Ellery. How the fuck did you get this number?"

"That's for me to know and you to wonder about. You need to get that fine ass of yours over here to get me. Another body has shown up."

"What? What body? How do you know about this before I do?"

"I have a few useful contacts."

"I'll just bet you do. Fine, I'm on my way once I decide how I'm going to explain this to Landry."

"Good luck with that. I'll be waiting in the hotel lobby. No need to come in, I'll look out for you."

"Wonderful." Gage hung up to the sound of Ellery's chuckles. "Sonofabitch. That man couldn't be more of a pain in the ass if he tried."

Gage dragged himself to the bathroom to splash cold water on his face. He ran damp fingers through his hair and repressed the urge to swear some more. His reflection showed him bloodshot eyes and a jaw shaded by stubble. He shook his head in disgust then retreated to the bedroom to find a sweater. If he was going to be dragging his ass all over the city into the night hours, he was at least going to be warm. He donned boots and a windbreaker before making his way down to the store. Landry was busy with a customer but spotted him right away. His smile gave way to a frown, which then morphed into a pouty scowl. He gave himself a shake and returned to his customer, apologizing for his lack of attention before completing his wrapping. Once the happy buyer had departed, Landry rested his hands on his hips and pinned Gage with a gaze worthy of any Dom.

"I've gotta go, love." To Gage's surprise Landry ran to him then gave him a smacking kiss and a hug.

"Be safe."

"I thought you'd be mad."

"Oh, I am but I'm not sending you out there worrying about how I'm feeling. I'm mad with the job, not with you. I'll deal. Expect to come back to me comatose on the couch, smeared with chocolate."

Gage gulped as he pictured Landry, naked and chocolaty. "That's not helping my composure one bit."

"Just reminding you what you have to come home to." Landry nibbled Gage's earlobe. "It's motivational."

"Jesus." Gage was inclined to toss Landry over his shoulder then carry him off to bed for a sound fucking. It took a few long, deep breaths before he convinced himself that his paycheck had to be earned. Landry's wicked grin told Gage he knew exactly what effect he was having.

"You are such a brat."

"It takes practice."

"Don't wait up, okay?"

"You can think of me in bed, humping your pillow."

"That's it. You're not to come until I give you permission."

"But that's so mean!"

"No touching, Landry. I'll know if you do."

Landry stamped his foot. "Then you have to get home real fast."

"Gonna lock you in chastity for a week." Landry gasped. "Plug you too."

"Stop it! You're getting me hard!"

"Uh huh. What goes around comes around."

"Go fight criminals. I'm counting this debate a draw."

"If you say so. You still don't get to come." On that note, Gage made a hasty exit, satisfied that he'd taken Landry's mind off any potential danger Gage might be walking into.

He'd barely pulled up in front of James Ellery's hotel when Ellery strolled out to join him. Gage steered back into traffic before speaking.

"I called in to the precinct on the way over. This isn't looking good."

"Bring me up to speed. I only heard that a body had been found near an antiques store, I don't know anything else." Ellery settled into his seat, relaxed and completely at home.

"You shouldn't even know that much, but whatever. Location is a place called Josephine's. It's a well-established, mid-range antique dealer that's been in the same location for close to twenty years. Proprietor is one Josephine McKay. An import from Scotland — came over here with her parents as a child."

"Is she the victim?"

"Don't know. The only information I have is that the deceased is female, mid-fifties, and has multiple stab wounds. She was found in an alley behind the store. We need to talk to the first responders at the scene and pick up the case. The antique store connection is too much of a coincidence to keep this separate from the other case."

"Could just be a mugging." Ellery didn't sound convinced.

"Could be." Gage didn't want to jump to conclusions either.

When they arrived, Gage left the Jeep behind a row of black and whites. Someone had taped off the alley and a small group of people were a few steps beyond it. Gage flashed his badge at the cop guarding the barrier before he and Ellery joined the group. Gage recognized the officer in charge as someone he knew.

"Hey, Craig, nice night for a crime."

"Gage Roskam, as I live and breathe. When the precinct told me you were on the way, I thought that couldn't be right. Thought you had to be dead by now."

"Against all expectations, here I am, still breathing the fine Seattle air."

"James Ellery." James held out a hand, which Craig shook, looking bemused.

"We so short of cops we're importing Brits now?" Craig addressed his question to Gage.

"He's not a cop. Craig Burgess, meet James Ellery. He's assisting with an investigation I'm working on. I'm stuck with him for now, sadly."

"He loves me really." Ellery peered down the alley. "Do we have an ID yet?"

"As a matter of fact we do," Craig replied. "We found the victim's purse in one of the dumpsters. Seemed to have been slung in there because it wasn't hidden or anything, it was just resting on top of the garbage. Name is Sarah-Lu Clancy, resident of this fair city, aged fifty-three. She had business cards in her purse which say she was the manager at a place called Number 51, which in case you didn't know is another —"

"Antique store," Gage interjected. "I know it. Well fuck. That makes the mugging theory less likely."

"That and her wallet was in her purse with three hundred dollars and some change in it. Her cell is in there too. She's wearing a lot of classy jewelry and an Omega watch."

"Who found the body?"

"Kitchen porter from a restaurant on this block was bringing out bags of garbage and spotted her. He called it in. Patrol guys were here in less than five minutes so it's safe to say the scene wasn't disturbed."

"Okay, we'll start with him but I guess he's not going to tell us much more." Gage rubbed the back of his neck as he glanced around. "No reason on this earth why the lady would be down a skanky alley miles away from her place of business. I'd put a few dollars on her having been killed elsewhere then dumped here."

James nodded. "Same as the man who was found outside Treasure Trove. This killer has a routine. I think he's sending a message, and he's not trying to hide behind a fake mugging."

"The press are here," Gage muttered. "This will be all over the papers tomorrow. Shit, it's probably already splashed across the Internet."

"Instant publicity—the curse of the modern-day policeman." James wrinkled his nose. "It could smell better back here. Why don't you go ask your questions, and I'll take a look at the front of the store?"

"And why don't you keep your suggestions to yourself? I'm in charge, not you." Gage shook his head as Craig gave him an amused look.

"Your Landry will have your balls if he finds out you have another boyfriend."

Ellery broke into peals of laughter, drawing stares from the small gathering of reporters and rubber-neckers behind the crime scene tape. "Good Lord, that's too funny."

Gage sighed. "Craig, I've already had a day and a half. Do you really need to make it worse? I'm gonna have nightmares tonight now."

Craig chuckled. "I'm gonna leave the two of you to your little spat. Jesus, I always assumed being gay would be less work than being with a woman."

"He's not, we're not… No way, not ever. Hell would not only have to freeze over, the polar bears would be partying down there before he and I got together."

Craig held up his hands. "Okay, okay, I get the message. It was nice seeing you, Gage. Be sure to pass my best on to Landry."

"I'll do that. Now go give grief to some other poor mug." Gage scowled at Ellery. "*You* go check out the street and the storefront."

"What a great idea. If only I'd thought of that."

Gage itched to reach for his gun. In his humble opinion, James Ellery would be greatly improved by a couple of bullet holes, but the Brit had already walked away.

"Fuck my life." Gage stared daggers at anyone who dared make eye contact, then got to work.

Chapter Eight

After three hours outside in progressively cooling weather, Gage was running on empty, his last nerve frayed. Examining the scene, talking to the CSIs, interrogating the guy who had had the misfortune to find the body… None of it gave Gage anything he didn't already know. Ellery came up empty too and there were signs that his normally ice-cold demeanor was edging toward impatience. Gage pulled him to one side. "We're getting nowhere fast. Other than confirming she was killed elsewhere, which we already assumed, we're not going to find any more useful information. It's time to regroup. We both need a decent night's sleep."

"Agreed. And I need to invest in some thermal underwear."

"The antique connection is making me nervous, I don't mind admitting."

"I don't blame you. Landry isn't stupid though. All that blond fluff hides a sharp mind."

"Don't I know it? I'm going to have to tell him about you and I'm not looking forward to that conversation."

"I could let you off the hook, drop into the store."

"He'll work it out. He'll know you were already here and he'll know that I've been with you…"

"And your balls will be the prettiest shade of blue."

"Don't even joke about that. You have no business thinking about my balls anyway. Oh my God, I must be even more tired than I thought. The direction of this conversation is the stuff of nightmares."

"I can get a cab back to my hotel," Ellery offered, his gaze softening.

"No, why would I subject some other poor resident of this fair city to you? Go get in the Jeep, just stop talking."

Ellery pulled a bag of jellybeans from his pocket. He offered them to Gage who shrugged before taking a handful.

"See, I'm not all bad."

"You're the only person on the street with that opinion."

Gage survived the drive across town, left Ellery at his hotel with a promise to pick him up first thing in the morning then returned to Treasure Trove. It was after midnight, and he was extra careful to relock gates and doors as he made his way from the street to the apartment. He let himself in, kicking off his shoes just inside the door in an attempt to be quiet. The glow of lamplight drew him to the living room where he found Landry curled into the corner of the couch, his head resting on the arm, covered with a pile of fluffy blankets. He was asleep but, as if he had sensed Gage's presence, he stirred.

"Gage, you're home." He didn't even open his eyes.

"I am." Gage crossed the room. He scooped Landry, blankets and all, into his arms before marching to the bedroom. "You shouldn't have waited up. It's late."

"I ate the chocolate," Landry mumbled, still not quite awake.

"I wouldn't have expected anything else." Landry proved to be completely bare beneath the blankets, and Gage luxuriated in the heat of his soft skin as he settled him into bed. Gage was exhausted and didn't contemplate a shower, deciding he'd probably drown. He stripped, dropping his clothes where he stood, then slipped beneath the comforter. In an instant, Landry had wiggled against him, nestling his ass in Gage's crotch, their skin touching from thigh to chest. Gage slung an arm around Landry's slender body, pulling him even closer.

"I'm here now. Sleep, baby." He wasn't sure if the words of comfort were for Landry or himself.

* * * *

Landry awoke with a sense of safety he only got from sharing a bed with Gage. He had a vague memory of Gage returning home then being carried to the bedroom but after that, nothing. *No sexy time. Need to do something about that.* It was early. The light coming through a chink in the drapes had the clear golden quality that came with dawn, but Landry knew Gage would have set the alarm for an ungodly hour. He always worked ridiculously long days when he had a new case, so Landry wriggled beneath the covers, nosing his way down Gage's chest, across his belly to the curls covering his groin. A subtle change in Gage's breathing told Landry he was awake. *His cock certainly is.* He gave Gage's stiffening shaft a lick. "Yum!"

"Landry…" Gage's voice was rough as gravel, and it sent a happy shiver down Landry's spine.

Right. Get on with it. Landry set to with relish, using all the tricks in his arsenal to ensure he worked Gage up to a frenzy. He knew all the things Gage loved best, from gentle nips with his teeth to long, slow sucking. He paid special attention to the head of Gage's dick, which was producing bead after bead of pre-cum. Landry lapped at it, Gage's essence coating his tongue. When Gage wound his fingers into Landry's hair, Landry grinned. It would only be a matter of time before Gage wouldn't be able to resist taking control and he was living up to Landry's expectations.

For a few seconds, Gage held Landry in place then he loosened his grip enough that Landry could take Gage's girth into his mouth. Landry ducked his head low, taking all of him, controlling his gag reflex with effort. He swallowed then moaned as Gage pulled his hair hard enough to sting. Gage's release came a moment later and Landry swallowed, content that he'd satisfied his Dom. His cock was hard and aching, but he didn't touch it before emerging from beneath the covers to plant a kiss on the end of Gage's nose.

"Good morning, Sir!"

"Could be worse." Gage grinned.

"Sir!"

"Come here." Gage pulled him down for a cuddle. "That was a perfect start to the day. Thank you."

"Any time." Landry placed a series of small kisses across Gage's chest.

"You didn't touch yourself last night, did you?"

"No, Sir. I used chocolate as a substitute for orgasms."

"How much chocolate did you eat exactly?"

"A lot."

"So when I came home, you were in a sugar coma."

"Probably. I was warm and dozy but I didn't want to go to bed without you."

"You were adorable in your blanket cocoon."

"I'm always adorable, Sir."

"I think it's best we not go there. I have to go to work, but first, kneel up. Get yourself off. I want to watch you come."

"Oh!" Landry scrambled into position straddling Gage's thighs. He fisted his cock—so close to coming he had to hold his breath.

"Slowly."

Landry let his breath out with a huff. "Please…" It was hard to get words out. "Please, Sir!"

"Do you want to come, sweetheart?"

"Oh God." Landry squeezed his eyes shut. He didn't dare move his hand anymore.

"I'll take that as a yes."

"Is that permission, Sir?"

"It is."

Two tugs and Landry came over his hand, Gage's thighs and the bed covers. The pleasure was so intense it was painful, his dick too sensitive.

"Nice." Gage twirled a finger through the pearls of cum on his leg.

"I needed that so bad." Landry collapsed so he lay on Gage's chest.

"You are a needy boy."

"I am."

"Go clean up. I have something to ensure you don't feel neglected while I'm working this case."

Landry propped his chin in his hands. "You wouldn't."

"You know I would."

"What if I lie here and refuse to move?"

"I'll most likely lose the key. If you move your butt, I'll let you choose which cage you get to wear."

"If I hadn't recently had a spectacular orgasm, I might run away."

"I'd track you down. Remember, I'm a detective. You couldn't get far enough before I'd catch you and drag your ass back to where I keep the handcuffs."

Landry contemplated for a minute or two and realized that Gage was right. "I should have done track at school. Who knew running could be a valuable skill?"

He hauled himself off Gage, out of bed and the short distance to the bathroom, muttering all the way. Having dealt with sticky substances, he returned to the bedroom to find that Gage had laid two chastity devices on the covers. Landry gave a loud, dramatic sigh.

"You meant it then?" One of the devices was stainless steel, the other clear acrylic. Landry had worn both before and couldn't say he'd enjoyed either, though his masochistic streak was definitely turned up to full. The physical manifestation of handing full control of his body to Gage was the stuff his kinky dreams were made of. "Lucky me, a choice."

"I know, I'm far too indulgent, and considering I haven't had either coffee or breakfast yet, you should count yourself lucky." Gage patted the bed. "Come kneel on here."

Pouting, Landry obeyed. "Is this a trick, where I pick one but you use the other?"

"So much cynicism in one so young."

"That one." Landry picked the acrylic. It was lighter—the metal one was difficult to forget. To his relief, it was the one he'd chosen that Gage locked into place, putting the key in the small tray he used to hold his collection of dimes.

"There, now you'll feel me with you every minute of the day."

Landry gave his groin a baleful glare. "So mean." He wormed beneath the covers. "So I'm going to gloat about being able to stay in bed a bit longer, while you have to go to work."

"I have a large collection of plugs…"

Landry debated his life choices. "Would you like me to make you some coffee, Sir?"

Gage chuckled. "Nice save, but no. I'll get takeout from Mary's place. I need to run."

Landry sulked a little as he listened to Gage banging around in the bathroom. With the covers pulled up to his nose he watched Gage dress, experiencing a pang of regret as each piece of skin was covered.

"Enjoying the show?" Gage ran a hand through his dark hair and his blue eyes glinted.

"Absolutely." Landry yelped as Gage yanked back the covers, exposing him.

"Then I should get my entertainment too, shouldn't I?" Before Landry even registered what was going on, Gage sat on the side of the bed then pulled him across his lap. He gave him half a dozen firm spanks while Landry squirmed and yelped, then he parted Landry's ass cheeks and rubbed a finger over his hole. In its prison, Landry's dick attempted to harden. "Like that, don't you? You'll be thinking about this for the rest of the day and every time you do, your poor, sweet cock will remind you what it means to be mine."

Landry was so turned on he didn't know what to do with himself. He wanted Gage to fill him, he wanted his fingers, his cock, but at the same time, he didn't because he knew what torment it would be. Gage rolled him off his lap onto the bed, and he lay there in a boneless heap.

"A pink butt suits you. I should keep it that way all the time."

Landry groaned. He didn't know what had brought on Gage's sudden frenzy of dominance, but he liked it.

"Have a nice day, sweetheart."

Gage was gone before Landry could summon up any kind of sarcastic retort. His backside glowed with a pleasant heat and his dick was still making a gallant effort to get hard. The acrylic casing around his shaft was tight, and Landry willed his erection away with mental images of Mr. Lao practicing tai chi in a pair of Superman boxers. There was no way he was going to be able to get back to sleep so he gave up with poor grace and grumbled his way to the shower.

Once he was clean and dressed, Landry decided to go for breakfast at the café. It was still too early to open the store, so he texted Petey to let him know what he was doing and to ask him what he wanted bringing back from Mary's. "I'll bet *he* doesn't have his dick locked up," Landry muttered as he made his way to the café. He was still talking to himself when he reached the counter.

"Wow, you're in here early," Mary said. "What can I get you, Landry?"

"Gage had to get up at ridiculous o'clock to go to work. Stupid dead bodies."

"Okay, Mr. Grumpy Pants, how about a nice fresh chocolate croissant and an extra-large, extra-frothy vanilla latte?"

Landry bounced. "That sounds perfect."

"I thought it might. Go grab a table. I'll bring them over."

Landry spotted Elton sitting in the corner by the window. He ambled over. "Hey, Elton, mind if I join you?"

"Sure thing. Mary's too busy to take a break at the moment."

"Cool." Landry plopped himself down on a chair, yawning. "I guess you're used to early starts."

"Sure am. I'm not working today though, but the habit's hard to break. I'm taking Mary out once she finishes the breakfast rush. Any news on the dead guy?"

"Not yet." Landry flapped his hands at Mary as she approached with his drink and croissant. "Gimme, gimme."

"Your coffee addiction is becoming a problem, young man. Not that I mind, you keep me in profit." Mary handed over his goodies. Landry took a big bite of flaky, chocolaty goodness then washed it down with a gulp of coffee, which was the perfect temperature. "So good," he moaned.

Mary and Elton exchanged amused glances. "Why do I feel like a voyeur?" Elton said. "Do you think I should leave him alone with that coffee?"

Mary giggled. "He certainly seems to be enjoying himself."

Landry rolled his eyes. "A man deserves some privacy with his first coffee of the day, don't you think?" Shaking her head, Mary went back to the counter where a line of caffeine-hunting customers had formed. "You and Mary seem to be hitting it off fine, Elton."

"She's a wonderful woman," Elton said. "I never thought a girl like her would give me the time of day."

"Why not?" Landry was mystified. "If you weren't straight, I'd lust after you."

"Good to know. I'm on a garbage crew. Most women ain't interested in someone in my profession."

"It's important work. Mary knows a good guy when she meets one." Landry chugged down some more coffee. "You have nothing to worry about. I've seen the way she looks at you."

"We're taking things slow and easy. I don't wanna frighten her off by rushing."

Knowing Mary, Landry guessed she might enjoy a bit of rushing, but he didn't say anything. "Well, for what it's worth, I think you make a great couple."

"How did you and the detective meet?"

"He was working a case. He insulted me and bought me baked goods."

"That would work."

"Of course, it also helps that he's one big hunk of gorgeousness." Landry raised his takeout cup for a toast, and Elton tapped their cups together.

"Here's to finding the one for you."

"Back at you." Landry glanced at the clock on the wall behind the counter. "I guess I should go open up. Antiques won't sell themselves. I hope you guys have a good day."

"You too. See you soon, Landry. Tell your detective I hope he solves this case. No one should get dumped like that, people aren't trash."

"You're so right." Landry checked his cell. "Must pick up Petey's breakfast order, and I think I need another coffee."

"Good Lord above, you must have caffeine in your veins."

"You say that like it's a bad thing. I think there's some residual blood in there, but I'm working on it." Landry blinked and headed for the counter.

Chapter Nine

Landry was still debating Elton's philosophical comment as he made his way back to Treasure Trove and went through his store opening routine. As he lifted the security shutter, he couldn't help but think of what Elton had said. Had Penton been dumped like so much trash or had his positioning in Treasure Trove's doorway been deliberate? Landry suspected the latter.

He had not long turned around the open sign when Petey stumbled through the door from the back hall.

"Sorry, sorry! I'm here." He lurched over to the cash desk, where Landry caught him as he tripped over a brass umbrella stand. "Sorry! Not awake."

"No kidding. What did you and Carson get up to last night? Your peppermint tea and bagel are in front of your nose, in case you can't see them, though that tea is real stinky."

Petey groped for the cup then took a few sips. "Oh, hot! Mary makes the best peppermint tea, although Mr. Lao comes a close second."

Landry shook his head. "You're a lost cause. Now spill. How come you're in such a state?"

"Has Gage ever used a press on you?" Petey spoke in a whisper.

"Fruit press, French press, garlic press, press-ups?" Landry grinned.

"None of those and I think you know exactly what I'm talking about."

"You mean a ball press." Landry didn't lower his voice.

"Hush, not so loud."

"There's no one in here but us, Petey."

"I know but I don't really want to shout about getting my balls squished between acrylic plates."

"You're such a pain slut. Carson spoils you."

"He does. This was a new design which had these metal spikes that you could screw in once it was on. It hurt so good then he fucked me while I was wearing it. I came like Old Faithful."

Landry shifted uncomfortably and focused on his second cup of coffee. "No talking about orgasms."

"Why…? Oh. Did Gage lock you up again?"

"He did. Meanest Dom ever and I need something to take my mind off my…predicament."

"How about we do some more research into the antiques that came over from the estate sale?"

"You're a bad influence. Gage told me not to get involved."

"A bit of web surfing is hardly getting involved."

"Okay. Bring up the catalog we downloaded, let's scan that first and see if inspiration strikes."

"Okay."

"I had a thought," Landry said.

"Careful now, sounds dangerous." Petey ducked Landry's swipe at his head.

"I do occasionally have one. Now I've lost my thread…oh yeah, the thought. If, and I guess it's a big if, the contents of the estate sale are important in some way, I was wondering why. Have I ever shown you my puzzle box?"

"The one with all the stages you have to go through to get it open?"

"That's the one. It's Japanese."

"Gage should keep the key to your chastity device in there."

"Do *not* suggest that to him. Ever. I would have to disown you."

"But you know how to get it open."

"I can never remember, it takes me ages and my brain would be all fuzzy from orgasm denial. I'd die of frustration."

"Drama queen much?"

"I…never mind, you're distracterating me."

"What even is that?"

"A new word. I like it."

"The box, Lan."

"Oh…right. It got me to thinking about things being hidden and I wondered if something was hidden in an item from the sale."

"Wouldn't people look over what they bought though?"

"Yeah but…you know that Nick Cage film, *National Treasure*?"

"Haven't watched it for a while, but yes."

"In it, the Resolute desk in the Oval Office had a secret compartment."

"But that's not true, that desk doesn't have any secret drawers or anything."

"So not where I'm going with this. Concentrate. I'm illustrating a point here. What if something from the sale *does* have a secret compartment? And what if there's something in it that someone, our murderer, doesn't want found?"

"That's quite a stretch and please don't call the psycho 'our' murderer."

"I still think we should check the catalog for likely candidates." Landry wasn't going to let Petey dampen his enthusiasm for treasure hunting.

"Okay, but I think there's a bunch of customers headed our way, so it'll have to wait."

"Well dang." Landry eyed the gaggle of ladies that had made their way into the store. "Anyone would think we were here to sell stuff."

Due to dealing with a steady stream of eager antique seekers, Landry didn't get a chance to examine the estate sale catalog until late in the afternoon. He scanned the list, discounting anything easy to investigate. A vase did not make the best hiding place. "Ooh, Petey, come look at this." Petey wandered back from the door where he'd been helping a customer carry an oak bookcase to his van.

"Whatcha got?"

"A prime candidate for secret hidey holes."

"Lemme see." Petey nudged Landry to one side. "This thing? What's a secretary cabinet?"

"A kind of fancy writing desk. What's important about this one though is it says it's in the style of Roentgen."

"I'm not following. Ex-cycle courier here remember. I'm years behind you learning all the antique stuff. Who was Roentgen?"

"He was an eighteenth-century German cabinet-maker, famous for marquetry and his secret drawers and mechanical fittings. He was around at the time of the French revolution and the Napoleonic wars. Mr. Lao told me he was a buddy of Marie Antoinette."

"Didn't she get her head chopped off?"

"Yep. Though she wanted the peasants to eat cake so she can't have been all bad." Landry grinned.

"You're an idiot. I don't think that was a good thing at the time. Still not getting the link here."

"Petey, he was famous for building mechanical secrets into his pieces. From the picture it looks like this desk is a slightly cut down copy of the Berlin secretary desk that Roentgen made for King Frederick William the second. It was on display once in an exhibition at the Metropolitan Museum of Art. There's probably a video somewhere."

Landry did a Google search for the desk and sure enough, there was a video of the various secret compartments opening, including an amazing easel, which unfolded at the end.

"Wow. That's remarkable." Petey was entranced.

"Isn't it? The one in the catalog must be a copy, which means that some of the secret compartments may have been copied too. Which means…"

"Something could be hidden in it!"

"And there's the home run!"

"You're gonna need to tell Gage about this, and he's either going to give you a thank you fuck or beat your behind."

"I've already had one spanking today. I could do without another." Landry drummed his fingers on the cash desk. "Perhaps I should call him, soften him up a bit." The instant he quit speaking, Landry's cell rang. He glanced at the screen. "It's Gage. He has this place bugged, I know he does."

"He so does." Petey grabbed the feather duster and began wafting it over random pieces of furniture.

"What are you doing? We've already cleaned today and I'm having a crisis." Landry answered the call.

"If there's bugs, there's cameras," Petey muttered, flicking rainbow feathers as if his life depended on it.

"Hey, Gage," Landry said. "You must be a mind reader. I was thinking about calling you."

"Why, nothing's wrong is it?"

"Why do you always automatically assume that something is going wrong when I call you?"

"You're seriously asking me that question? Just tell me there isn't another dead body anywhere near you."

"Not at the moment, though Petey is skating a bit close to the edge." Petey danced past, slapping his butt to some imaginary tune. "Why are you calling? You're just as likely to get into trouble as I am."

"Am not."

"Am so."

"If you want to stand any chance at all of getting out of that chastity cage, you're going to stop this debate right now, young man."

"You always pull the Dom card," Landry whined.

"Never gonna stop taking advantage of that." Gage laughed.

"Seriously, why are you calling?"

"To give you a heads-up that I'm bringing this Brit they've foisted on me back for dinner."

"Oh, cool. I was planning tacos for dinner tonight. Is that still okay?"

"Sure, he'll eat what he's given and like it."

"Not loving the new partnership then?"

"Well… It's not exactly new. I'll explain this evening. Gotta go."

"Wait! What do you mean it's not new? Gage… Well fuck, he's gone." Landry waved Petey over. "I get the feeling I'm going to be off the hook this evening. Gage sounded so guilty. I think he's done something much worse than a little bit of sneaky research."

"Why, what did he say?"

"Just that he's bringing the Brit that he's working with on this case over for dinner." Landry frowned, a kernel of doubt forming in his mind. "It can't be, can it?"

"Can't be what? I'm good at cryptic crosswords, but interpreting your thought processes sometimes… They are indecipherable."

"Who was the last Brit that crossed our paths?"

"That blond guy, James Ellery. The one who was dating the boy linked to the Japanese Yakuza and then turned out to be behind your last treasure hunt."

"The one that kidnapped me, you mean, and all to get his mitts on a valuable necklace. Then he planted my mirror so I'd find clues to hidden treasure and do his work for him. *That* Brit. There are good reasons why the best movie villains are British, you know."

"The accent? No wait, don't tell me… Something to do with the Boston tea party? We threw tea in the harbor and they've hated us ever since."

"They are stupid crazy about tea, but no. Nor is it the fact that they can't spell or that for some reason they call jelly jam. No, I'm convinced it's because most of them drive stick shifts."

Petey gave him a puzzled look. "What has that got to do with inherent evilness?"

"It's complicated. Unnecessarily complicated. All that thinking when they drive has addled their brains and turned them evil."

"If you say so. Seems as good an explanation as any. Personally, I would have put it down more to the whole colonialism take-over-the-planet thing but that's just me. Anyway, you can't be thinking that Gage's new partner is James Ellery?"

"That's exactly what I'm thinking. If he's already working with that…that *person* and he hasn't told me, he's going to be sleeping on the couch."

"I get why you'd be pissed about that, but isn't making him sleep on the couch punishing yourself?"

"Hmm, you have a point. I need to think of something else, some other way to punish him."

"How about waiting to see if it really is him? It's a chance in a million. He could be entirely innocent. You're probably stressing out over nothing."

"You're right. I'm being an idiot. Ellery is probably burglarizing some high-rise in Hong Kong or breaking into the Tower of London or something. That's more his speed. And knowing him, if he got caught with the Crown Jewels he'd convince the authorities he was doing the Queen a favor."

Petey chuckled. "You really don't like him, do you?"

"He just rubs me the wrong way." Landry sighed and adjusted his pants. "Not that I'm getting rubbed in any kind of interesting way at the moment."

"You should wait until Gage takes that thing off you before you scold him."

"He is far too fond of locking up my dick. And spanking my ass. And tying me up. I love him so much!"

"You're crazy. We should all have a night out at Scorch soon. I got their last newsletter and there was an article in it about a new bondage wheel, which looks like so much fun."

"What's that then? I thought my mental catalog of bondage equipment was quite complete."

"What's your favorite Duran video?"

"Same as yours. *Wild Boys*. Whoever thought that up was definitely kinky."

"And Simon Le Bon is…"

"Strapped to a wheel that dips his head into the water. Oh, *that* kind of wheel."

"I don't think there's any water involved, but yes. There are loads of straps to keep you safely in place and then it spins. It's operated by a foot pedal and it can be locked into several different positions. It's on a platform so if you're turned completely upside down, your dick would be at the perfect height for your Dom to get slurping."

"I don't think I'd like being upside down," Landry said. "I went on a rollercoaster once that did a loop-the-loop and when I got off I threw up in a trash can. I wouldn't mind watching you though."

"It didn't say whether it was in a private room, or in a public area."

"I bet if it's new, it'll be out in the main club. The crowd will want somebody to get inventive with it."

"Carson doesn't mind people watching as long as they don't touch, and I don't care. I forget there's anyone there apart from him when we're in a scene. We could be in the middle of Lumen Field and I'd be none the wiser. Sub space is dreamy."

"I'm sure if you talk to him about it, he'll be dragging you down there in an instant."

"You and Gage will come too, won't you?"

"It has been ages since we had a night out. I'll ask him tonight. He can talk to Carson and fix a date."

Petey whooped and danced down the aisle singing *Wild Boys* completely off key. Landry shook his head. "Good Lord, that's offensive. Put the closed sign on the door while you're down there. It's time we were locking up."

Chapter Ten

"Well, that was an absolute shit show of a day," Gage proclaimed to no one in particular as he parked the Jeep around the corner from Treasure Trove. In the passenger seat, James Ellery grunted.

"Though I wouldn't have chosen precisely those words, I can't disagree. It felt like we were walking on shale, two steps forward, one long, slow slide backward narrowly avoiding landing on our asses."

"And it's about to get worse. Be warned, Landry is making tacos and that means he has the heavy skillet out. I wouldn't be at all surprised if it connected with your head not long after we get into the apartment."

"Not going to happen. Landry loves me."

"He loves you about as much as he loves spinach and if you'd seen the faces he makes when he has to eat it, you'd understand."

"Spinach is good for him and so am I. Deep down, he knows that."

"I dare you to say that to his face."

"I think we should let him warm up to me gradually, don't you?"

"Ellery, you're here under sufferance. I didn't ask to work with you and my tolerance is already stretched to the breaking point. You do anything, anything at all, to upset Landry more than he's already going to be, and I will shoot you."

"I do enjoy a nice threesome. Perhaps I should suggest that. I'm sure Landry would relish a little spit roasting." Gage reached for his gun. "Joke! I'm joking. You are so easy to rile."

"And you are skating on very thin ice. I'm sending you into the apartment first. If Landry starts throwing things, I'm using you as a human shield." Gage got out of the Jeep. Ellery tracked him as he went through the routine of unlocking the outside gate, crossing the courtyard and heading into the back of Treasure Trove. Gage took care to ensure everything was locked behind him.

"This case is a bit close to home, isn't it?" Ellery said.

"I don't like the antique connection, that's for sure," Gage replied. "With the first body being dumped here, there has to be a link somewhere. We just haven't found it yet."

He stomped up the stairs, feet dragging through a mixture of reluctance to face Landry and the fatigue brought on by a long, frustrating day. He unlocked the apartment door then shoved Ellery in. The lack of projectiles gave him courage so Gage followed behind and he could hear Landry clattering around in the kitchen.

"We're here, sweetheart."

"Hi, Sir. Hello, James."

Gage exchanged a startled glance with Ellery. "Oh, fuck. He already worked it out."

Landry emerged from the kitchen holding his biggest, sharpest knife. "I knew it. You would never call me 'sweetheart' when you had a guest with you unless you were trying to butter me up."

"How about you put the knife down, Landry?"

"I don't think so." Landry used it to scrape under a fingernail.

"Hi, Landry, nice to see you again." Ellery stayed exactly where he was.

"Look at the pair of you. Two big, fierce Doms scared of little old me. Come in and sit down for Christ's sake. There's a bottle of wine breathing on the table." He disappeared back into the kitchen, and Gage ushered Ellery through to the living room.

"Pour yourself a drink—I think you're going to need it." He left Ellery with the bottle before returning to the kitchen. "I should have known you'd work it out," he said, wrapping his arms around Landry from behind.

"You'd be completely useless at poker," Landry said, nestling his ass against Gage's groin. "I could hear the guilt in your voice when you called earlier, I didn't even need to see your expression and when you said it wasn't a new partnership, well, that limited the options, didn't it?" He jiggled the skillet, which was full of aromatic ground beef and onions.

"On a scale of one to ten, how mad are you?"

"On a volcano scale, I'm somewhere between Mount St. Helens and Kilimanjaro. I haven't quite reached Vesuvius yet."

"Thank the Lord for small favors."

"I was talking to Petey earlier and convinced myself it couldn't possibly be true but once I was alone, the more I mulled it over, the more convinced I was. I guess you didn't ask to work with him."

"Are you kidding me? Of course not. I was saddled with his annoying ass, as I said. If it helps, he did save my life."

"What?" Landry exclaimed.

"When I got clocked at the storage facility, Ellery scared off the guy that hit me. If he hadn't been there…"

"And you're sure it wasn't Ellery that hit you?"

"Quite sure. Different height and build."

"I still don't have to like him though, do I?"

"If you can manage not to damage him so much that he can't work, that would be helpful. With Sancha away, I hate to say it but I need him. He knows his stuff when it comes to antiques even if he does have a tendency to steal them."

"You like him despite yourself, don't you? He's grown on you."

"Like fungus."

Landry snickered. "I guess since he's here we'd better feed him. Go check he hasn't drunk all the wine. I need a glass. Badly."

"Just one for you. Two glasses and you lose all your inhibitions and you didn't have many of those to start with."

"Hey! Are you saying I'm a slut?"

"Only for me, sweetheart, only for me."

"You're gonna take this off tonight, aren't you?" Landry patted his groin.

"We'll see. If Ellery makes it out of here alive, I'll think about it."

"Who needs orgasms anyway?" Landry muttered under his breath. "Go. I'm going to lay this out on the table buffet-style. Then we can make up our own tacos."

Gage gave one of Landry's nipples a tweak. "Love you."

"Love you back."

Ellery had made himself at home on the couch. He had his eyes shut and was sipping his wine. "I poured you a glass. I wasn't sure if Landry would be allowed." He spoke without opening his eyes.

"Thanks to your presence, Landry is craving alcohol. I'll get it. We're having a serve yourself taco supper, so you'll have to haul your ass off the couch in a minute."

Ellery blinked, looking for all the world as if he'd awoken from a restful nap. "Sounds great."

Landry bustled in and out with an assortment of dishes. "Okay, it's all here. Nothing's poisoned, but, Gage, maybe you should take the food on this side."

"I appreciate your hospitality, at least I think I do. Ask me again in a few hours," Ellery said as he got to his feet. "It all looks delicious, Landry."

"Okay, that's enough," Landry said. "Acting the polite guest doesn't suit you. If you have to be here, no faking. Be yourself."

"Thank fuck for that," Ellery said. "Two sentences were already stretching the limits of my acting ability. How have you been, cute stuff? Did you miss me?"

"Gage, he called me cute. Shouldn't you be smacking him or something?"

"You are cute." Gage took a long swallow of wine. "And I'm not in the habit of beating up our guests."

"Can you make an exception?"

Ellery laughed then ruffled Landry's hair as he passed him on his way to the table. "I wasn't lying about food. I could eat a giraffe."

"Why would you...? Never mind. Eat. Try not to choke, because my first aid skills are minimal at best."

Once they'd all served themselves, Gage retreated to the couch. He pulled Landry onto his lap, and Ellery found a streak of diplomacy and took the separate armchair. The silence while they ate wasn't comfortable, but Gage was hungry and the loaded tacos were fantastic. He devoured four in the time it took Landry to eat two, and Ellery kept pace. Landry stared at both of them in turn.

"You guys are stress eating, right?"

"Absolutely," Ellery agreed. "Which is why I appreciate my good genes." He patted his flat stomach. "I can eat what I like and never gain a pound."

"I thought I couldn't dislike you any more, but I was wrong." Landry swallowed the rest of his wine. "I want to know about the case." He swiveled to face Gage. "You owe me that, bringing him here."

"You should tell him," Ellery said. "His mind works in peculiar ways—he could be useful."

"Hey! I am not peculiar!" Landry poked his tongue out at Ellery who shrugged and grinned. "And you can stop smirking." Landry prodded Gage's bicep.

Gage settled Landry more comfortably in his lap. "Fine, but bear in mind that if anything about me sharing gets back to the Bald Eagle, you're staying in chastity for a month."

"Oh, how delicious. You have him caged." Ellery lifted his glass in a toast. "It's no wonder you and I are friends."

"I can't believe I gave him tacos," Landry muttered. "Stop sucking up to my boyfriend and don't even think of referencing sucking in your next sentence."

"How about we stick to the case," Gage said, wondering whom he should gag first. "It'll be safer."

"I knew this evening would be entertaining." Ellery stretched out his legs, crossing them at the ankles.

"Give me strength. There's not enough wine in the world." Gage took a breath. "Okay, I'll give you the bare bones. So far we have five bodies."

Landry squeaked "Five? What the actual fuck?"

"No swearing. Three of them were in the U.K. On the surface, they looked like accidents, but Ellery is convinced that's not the case. They are all linked to a shipment of antiques that originated at an estate sale."

"At Crowberry Castle," Landry finished the sentence.

"Yes. I'm not going to ask how you know that when I specifically told you not to do any digging. And it's no good batting your lashes like that. You couldn't look innocent if you tried."

Ellery snickered. "You should tie him up more, keep him out of mischief."

"If I wanted your opinion, I'd ask for it." Gage scowled. "Though, you have a point."

"Hey!" Landry squirmed in Gage's lap.

"Do you want to hear about the case or not?"

"His fault." Landry sulked but kept quiet.

"So on this side of the pond, there have been two bodies so far. The first you know about, obviously. The second was discovered last night. Now the body was found in the alley behind Josephine Mackay's antique store, but she wasn't the victim—that was one Sarah-Lu Clancy who runs yet another store, Number 51."

"This is getting a little scary."

"Ellery thinks that there may be something hidden in an item from the estate sale which is evidence in the suspicious death of the castle's owner in England, though at the moment it hasn't been classed as a murder."

"I think that might be right," Landry said. "Now don't be mad, because I know you told me not to do any of the Scooby stuff, but I was only looking through the catalog from the estate sale, promise."

"We'll discuss a suitable punishment for disobedience later. Did you find anything useful?"

"I can think of some punishments you might enjoy handing out, Gage." Ellery's face was a picture of innocence.

"Such as?" Despite himself, Gage was interested. Ellery had a devious mind.

"We should talk. Predicament bondage is fascinating, don't you think?"

Landry's eyes widened. "Stop it! This is not a topic for discussion between the two of you. Get back to the case. Honestly, dead bodies are a safer subject."

Gage pushed his hand up the back of Landry's T-shirt to stroke warm, smooth skin. "Are you going to tell us what you found in the catalog?"

"Petey and I came to the same conclusion that you have, that there's something hidden in the shipment. A whole load of stuff was brought here to the States, but there's one piece that's particularly interesting. A secretary desk in the style of Roentgen."

"Why did that catch your interest?" Gage asked.

"Because Roentgen was a furniture designer famous for including hidden drawers and cupboards in his furniture," Ellery interjected. "I should have realized."

"So we need to track down who bought that particular piece of furniture and find out where it is now." Gage reached for the wine bottle to top up his glass. "I'm guessing that Arthur Penton shipped it over. That's why he was the first victim and why I ran into trouble at his storage facility. There'll no doubt be something in his books listing what he imported. I'll have to go back to the Antiquarium."

"But why was Sarah-Lu killed?" Landry asked.

"Well, if it is that particular piece of furniture our killer is looking for and he didn't find it at the storage facility, perhaps he thought she might know something about it. We'll have to look for a connection between her and Penton."

Ellery nodded. "We didn't get very far today. This should put us in the right direction."

"You mean I actually helped?" Landry asked.

"We'd have got there eventually, but you've saved us some time and somehow I think that's going to be important in this case," Gage replied.

"We should make an early start in the morning." Ellery got to his feet. "See me out, Gage, and I'll get a cab back to my hotel."

Gage wasn't going to argue. He didn't trust himself to drive after two glasses of wine in quick succession and he was tired. He wanted some quality time with Landry, not to be driving across the city. Gently, he lifted Landry onto the couch. "I want you waiting for me when I get back. You should take your clothes off."

Landry blushed. "Yes, Sir," he whispered.

"You're a very lucky man," Ellery said as Gage walked him out to the street.

"Go call Tad. You need some nice kinky phone sex." Gage hailed a passing cab. Ellery got in then opened the window. "I'll do that. Thinking about you and Landry together will keep me stimulated for a while." He winked, his smug expression disappearing as the window rose.

"Fuck my life," Gage muttered. "He'll be lucky if he gets through another day with me unscathed." He popped a couple of knuckles. "I really want to wipe that smile off his ridiculously handsome face." He stomped back to the gate into the yard, locking it behind him. "Now to deal with my cute but disobedient sub."

Chapter Eleven

Landry knelt on the bed waiting for Gage. He was a little nervous, in an excited, shivery kind of way. He'd been bad, but so had Gage, and he hadn't done any harm. He'd helped. He spread his legs wider and glared at the plastic encasing his cock. "You want out, don't you? I can't believe he locked you up again."

"It's a vicious cycle, isn't it?" Gage appeared in the doorway.

"What is, Sir? Talking to my dick?"

"That's you being you. No, I mean being in chastity excites you, which means you want out. The frustration gets you going even more. Me refusing to release you, keeping control…well, that's your fantasy, isn't it?"

Landry bounced his ass on his heels. "Not saying anything that might incriminate me, Sir."

"You don't have to. I know you, Landry Carran, inside and out. Did you prep for me?"

"Uh huh. Might have lubed a bit too." *A lot actually. Sue me, I was having fun.*

"Oh you did, did you? You had your fingers inside that sweet little hole. I don't think I gave you permission to do that."

"I was thinking of you, and you didn't say I couldn't."

"Sir."

"You didn't say I couldn't lube my hole, *Sir*." Landry batted his lashes.

"Did you just use your fingers or was a toy involved?"

"Uh, one of your dildos may have fallen out of the toy drawer."

"Did it, now? So, you pleasured yourself. Got all excited and made your poor dick swell in that cage. Probably tweaked your nipples a few times too, and all without me." Gage tutted.

"I had righteous justification. I was frustrated and you were running around the city with..."

"Don't say his name in the bedroom. I don't want him in my head while I'm fucking you." Gage stalked over to the bed. "He doesn't get to watch, even in my head. Every bit of you is mine."

Inside, Landry glowed with happiness. He loved when Gage got possessive. "I am. You make me all squirmy happy."

"Sir."

"I am yours, Sir. You're feeling especially Dommy tonight, aren't you? If that's the effect the not-to-be-named person has on you, I approve."

"It helps that you're kneeling naked on our bed. I'm very fond of you in that position. So what should I do with you?"

Landry blinked, suddenly much more self-conscious about being bare while Gage was fully dressed. "Fucking was mentioned, Sir." *Please, please, please with a nice shiny orgasm on top.*

"Punishment first."

"Aw, really?" Landry sighed. "Sir. I'd really like to get straight to the bit where you screw me into the mattress."

"I'm sure you would. Did you think you'd get away with disobeying me?"

"Yes?"

"Not gonna happen."

"So mean, Sir."

Gage gave one of his enigmatic smiles, which only served to make him more handsome, more desirable and more frustrating. He went to the toy drawer in the dresser, pulling out a set of padded handcuffs and a plug. Landry gulped.

"On your hands and knees, ass in the air." Gage's tone suggested there was not room for either negotiation or compromise.

Landry watched as Gage slathered the plug with a liberal coating of lube. He got into position, turning sideways to give Gage easy access. "I haven't seen that one before. Is it new?"

"It is. Something I picked up recently. I've been waiting for an opportunity to use it and now seems appropriate." Landry peered over his shoulder to get a closer look at the toy, which was bulbous and had an extended base. There was also a separate remote control. "Not only does it expand, it also vibrates. It should keep that overactive mind of yours busy while I fuck your mouth. But first, hands behind your back."

Landry had to turn his head sideways and press his cheek against the bed so that Gage could fasten the cuffs in place. There was a little slack in the chain that connected them, but not much. As soon as he'd secured Landry's hands, Gage pressed the plug to his hole. Having prepped earlier, Landry had no trouble taking it in, though he had to force himself to relax because he was so hyped. Once the plug was fully seated, the extended part of the base pressed hard against his perineum, causing all kinds of interesting sensations. Then Gage used the remote control and the plug expanded in Landry's channel, nudging against his prostate. He moaned, swamped by an excess of stimulation, and his dick fought to swell.

"Oh fuck!" Landry was at the point of using his safe word when the plug stopped inflating. The stretch was extreme and when Gage made the plug vibrate, turning the speed up in three increments, Landry howled. "No, yes, no!"

"You have a safe word, Landry. Use it if you need to."

Landry took several deep, gasping breaths. "So big, Sir!"

"Indeed. That's the point."

"Stop smirking, Sir."

"I've earned it. Now, sit on the edge of the bed so your mouth is at the right height to take my cock. I don't want to get a backache."

Landry scowled as he scrambled to do as Gage ordered, which wasn't easy with his hands bound. Sitting drove the plug deep and he gasped, finding it hard to focus on anything but his desperate need to come. Gage unzipped. He didn't undress, just released his cock and without ceremony pressed it to Landry's lips.

"Open your mouth and don't move. This is about me taking what I want." Gage took hold of Landry's hair with one hand and guided his rigid dick into his mouth with the other. Landry opened as wide as he could but otherwise remained still. Gage jacked his hips, slowly at first, then faster. Landry had to fight his gag reflex when the tip of Gage's cock touched the back of his throat. There was nothing he could do to escape the vibrations inside his body, nothing he could do to release his aching cock. All he could do was take what Gage gave him and he loved every second.

"So hot, not gonna last." Gage's grip on Landry's hair tightened. Landry's jaw ached. His eyes watered. If he hadn't been gagged by Gage's fat cock, Landry would have screamed.

"Yes!" Gage came, flooding Landry's mouth and throat. Gage didn't pull out right away and a few drips escaped Landry's mouth, dribbling down his chin. For several seconds, Gage remained frozen, then he shuddered before taking a step back. He smiled at Landry, brushed the tears from his cheeks then held up the remote and upped the speed on the vibrating plug.

"No!" Landry wailed. "It's too much."

"It's not supposed to be fun. Are you going to disobey me again, Landry?"

"No, sir! Well, probably yes... But I'll always confess, promise." Landry tipped forward in an attempt to take some of the pressure off his butt.

"I don't think you're quite getting the point here, Landry. You disobey me, you'll be punished. Every time, no exceptions."

"Yes, Sir, I mean no, Sir... I can't think."

He rolled onto his belly, drumming his feet on the bed. Slowly, Gage stripped. "Your problem is that you think too much. I'll take the plug out when I'm ready to fuck you. I suggest you put your mind to getting me hard again."

The glimmer of hope that Gage planted in Landry's mind was motivating. He wriggled and squirmed until he managed to get to his knees. Gage was standing next to the bed, gloriously naked.

"Your dick needs to get with the program," Landry muttered. "Come lie next to me."

Gage's eyes glittered with amusement. He lay down with his hands behind his head. "Go for it."

"Could you just switch off the…?"

"No. In fact there is a higher speed…" Gage reached for the remote.

"That won't be necessary," Landry squeaked. He ducked his head and began to lap at Gage's nipples. They peaked into hardness and a slight stiffening in Gage's posture told Landry that his tongue was working its magic. He headed south, tasting Gage's abs and his belly, then nosed his way down his treasure trail to the root of his cock. It was showing signs of life. "Excellent."

Landry gasped as his movements made the vibrating plug push harder against his prostate. "Fuck!"

"Not yet physically possible I'm afraid," Gage said.

"You are taking far too much delight in my situation," Landry muttered.

"Good. Maybe you'll think twice the next time you feel tempted to ignore my instructions."

"Never gonna let me forget that, are you?" Landry nudged at Gage's balls with his nose. He sucked, nibbled and teased until Gage's cock perked into life. Relieved, Landry gave Gage's shaft a few long licks.

"It's not a lollipop," Gage said. "Turn around."

Landry straddled Gage's thighs then bent forward, presenting him with the perfect view of Landry's ass. After a couple of stabs at the remote, the vibrations slowed then stopped and the plug deflated. Gage pulled it partway out but then shoved it back in. He repeated the process a few times while Landry squealed and protested. Finally, Gage removed it completely.

"I think you should do the work. Ride me."

Still facing away from Gage, Landry edged backward to align his hole with Gage's straining cock. With his hole slippery from lube, it took Landry several attempts to notch the tip of Gage's cock inside him. He sank down with a sigh, fuller than he had been even with the inflated plug.

"That's so pretty. Watching my cock disappear inside your body where it belongs."

"Thank you, Sir." Landry started to bounce, feeling the strain in his thighs and stomach muscles as he fought to keep his balance without the use of his hands. The chastity device was making its presence felt. Landry moved faster. He needed Gage to come. Gage however was not cooperating.

"So good. Keep going, sweetheart."

"A little help here?" Landry pleaded.

"Swivel around. I want to see your face." With Gage still inside him, Landry pivoted until he could look into Gage's eyes.

"Please, Sir."

"Since you beg so sweetly." Gage raised his knees and jerked his hips, ramming into Landry's body again and again. He tilted his head back, lips slightly parted, then came with a grunt of satisfaction. Heat filled Landry's channel and he kept moving, milking every last drop of Gage's orgasm. He slumped onto Gage's chest.

"Please let me come, Sir. I'll be good, I promise."

"Unlikely, but you can go get the key."

With undignified speed, Landry scrambled to reach Gage's change bowl. He realized that his hands were still bound and had to duck his head to pick up the keys in his mouth. He got back on the bed and dropped the keys on Gage's chest.

"I only want to keep you safe, you know that. There's a reason I don't want you mixed up in violent cases. I can't handle the thought that you might get hurt." He unlocked and removed the chastity device then took Landry's shaft in his hand.

Landry achieved an erection in record time and Gage tightened his grip. "I love you. I'll always love you, even though you are an unmitigated brat who causes me more stress than any number of criminals."

"I…" Landry forgot whatever it was he'd been about to say as Gage gave his dick a few tugs. Landry tried to hold back, but it was no good. His time in chastity had made him needy and desperate. He came into Gage's hand, the release so fierce it bordered on painful. He thrust into Gage's grip, his movements jerky and uncoordinated. His entire body was flushed with heat, and he shook as repeated spasms rolled down his spine. Finally, the tremors stopped and Landry sagged, exhausted. Gage pulled him down so that they were chest to chest and released him from the cuffs. Landry sprawled over him, needing skin-to-skin contact. Gage hugged him hard, stroking his ass.

"That was so good," Landry murmured. "Love you, Sir." It was hard to keep his eyes open. He couldn't summon the energy to make the trip to the bathroom so stayed where he was. If he and Gage got stuck together, then so be it. There were worse places to be.

Chapter Twelve

"Hey, Carson, if you're looking for Petey he's out buying our lunch. He won't be long." Landry beckoned Petey's boyfriend over to the cash desk. "You not on shift today?"

Carson pulled over a huge leather armchair that would have taken both Landry and Petey to move. He sank into it with a happy sigh. "I have three whole days off, starting now," he said. "Feels like forever since this part of my rotation has come round. How's business?"

"Good. We gained a bit of publicity when the news of the rare coin we found got out. Folks are curious. They drop in because they're nosy but often end up buying something. Mr. Lao thinks it's great because his retirement fund is growing by the day."

"My mom collects little glass animals, so if you ever get anything like that in, I've asked Petey to put them to one side. She loves Murano. Dust traps, all of them, but she has quite a collection and is always looking for new ones, birds especially."

"We have had one or two. I'll ask Mr. Lao to keep an eye out on his buying trips. I'm hoping he'll let me go with him one day. We really need someone else in the store though. It's hard work on your own, and I wouldn't want to leave Petey by himself."

The bell above the door rang, and Petey came in with his arms full of paper bags, juggling a cardboard tray of drinks. He dumped everything on the counter then threw himself into Carson's lap. Once he'd disengaged from a long, noisy kiss, he gave Landry a coy look.

"Sorry, it's been hours since we saw each other."

Landry rolled his eyes. "No kidding."

"I didn't get you anything to eat," Petey told Carson. "You're a bit earlier than I expected."

"Don't worry about it. I can head next door to pick something up, but I thought I'd catch you on your lunch break."

"Petey, why don't you take the afternoon off?" Landry suggested. "I can manage here by myself for a few hours and it's a beautiful day. You should take advantage."

"Really?" Petey bounced in Carson's lap. "That would be super cool. If you're sure you don't mind?"

"Go for it. In fact, I'll give Mr. Lao a call to see if he can come in the next two days so that you and Carson can spend some time together. You've covered for me often enough, you have some time owed."

"Wow! You're the best friend ever." Petey jumped from Carson's lap, ran to Landry and gave him a big kiss on the cheek. "But you'll tell me if Mr. Lao can't come in, won't you?"

"Sure. Get out of here."

"You're a good guy, Landry." Carson stood, towering over both of them. "Gage mentioned a night out at Scorch if you're up for it tomorrow?"

"I so am!" Landry bounced. "Gage might want to bring his temporary partner though."

"Yes, I heard that James Ellery is back in town. I guess if Gage can work with him without filling him with bullet holes, then I can manage a night at Scorch in his company. Hey, come to think of it, I've been wanting to practice my bullwhip skills on someone. He'd do."

Landry giggled. "I'd pay good money to watch that, but I don't think our Mr. Ellery likes being on the receiving end."

"Unlike me!" Petey said.

"I've told you, love, I need to get a lot more proficient with the whip before I go anywhere near you with it," Carson said. "But we can definitely try out that wheel you were talking about, and I have a nice, springy new cane."

"Ouch." Landry winced.

"I know, isn't it great," Petey enthused. "I can't wait."

Carson patted his head. "My sweet little masochist. Let's get outta here before Landry changes his mind."

Petey grabbed his lunch bag and drink, and the two of them walked arm in arm down the aisle, Petey chattering away. Landry smiled as he watched them go. He loved seeing his best friend so happy now that he'd found a man who could give him exactly what he needed.

For a while, Landry puttered around the store adjusting displays and moving older bits of stock into more prominent positions. He was fortunate that stock tended to have a quick turnover at Treasure Trove, but there were always one or two sticky pieces that took a while to shift. Often they were things that Mr. Lao had taken in as favors either to other dealers, friends or relatives. Landry had a talent for making even the ugliest piece of furniture look attractive in a window display. Today's item of choice was a particularly hideous chaise longue, which, although it had an attractive shape, had at some point in its life been upholstered in a very unfortunate choice of fabric. By the time Landry had finished with the display, the window looked like a room in a high-class brothel. He hummed his satisfaction as he worked, knowing that the dark red accessories and draped brocade would attract several of his regulars who he would then convince to see past floral chintz to the beauty of the piece beneath.

In an antique store, the cycle of dusting and polishing was never-ending, but Petey had already given the place a thorough clean that morning. The books were up-to-date, the website in order and invoices paid. With nothing urgent left to do, Landry's mind strayed to Gage's case. *I wonder if the order not to get involved was a one-time thing, because Gage didn't specifically say I couldn't do any research today. I'll take a little peek, that's all.* Landry settled behind the cash desk where he could keep an eye on the door then flipped open his laptop. *Now, how to go about tracking down a certain secretary desk.* He started by refreshing his memory, reading the description in the catalog. It made no mention of hidden drawers, but from the picture, Landry could see several possibilities where recesses or cavities might be hidden. *I need to check it out at the very least, then if I'm wrong, it's crossed off the list. Gage can't possibly complain about me calling another antique dealer to say hi.*

Landry searched for the number for Penton's Antiquarium. He dialed and it seemed to take forever to connect. It rang for so long that Landry kept expecting to be connected to voicemail, but just as he was about to disconnect, someone picked up.

"Penton's Antiquarium, this is Sorrell speaking. I'm afraid we're closed."

"Oh, hey… Sorry to bother you. I'm not a customer. I'm calling from Treasure Trove Antiques and I wondered if I'd be able to talk to somebody about a piece that you may have in stock?"

"I'm not sure," Sorrell said. "I'll try to help if I can but I'm only here clearing up a little. You may have heard… Something terrible happened to Mr. Penton. Wait, wasn't he found near your store?"

"Okay, I'm gonna come clean. My name is Landry Carran. I was the one who found the body."

"That must have been awful for you. I can't imagine… I would have been so scared."

"It wasn't the most fun time I've ever had. My partner is a detective working the case. I'm following up a lead."

"Oh, wow! You're with Detective Roskam. He's a hotty. I'm afraid we didn't make the best impression when he came by the store because we were celebrating Mr. Penton's demise. He wasn't a nice person. I do remember your detective saying that you and I would get on, though. I wasn't that drunk."

"Really? We should so get together for coffee. You do like coffee, right?"

"So long as it's accompanied by something sugary," Sorrell said.

"I think I may have found another soulmate." Landry giggled.

"I think I know your store. You're opposite a place called the Eastern Emporium, aren't you? And there's a cute coffee shop next door that does the most amazing pastries."

"That's us."

"You're so lucky. That's a great position. From here I have to walk three blocks just to get a decent cup of coffee."

"That is unfortunate. I hope they pay you enough in compensation."

"It's not so bad but I'm not sure about the future. With Mr. Penton gone, we don't yet know what's going to happen to the store. His mother is here looking over the accounts, but she's getting on, and I think she might end up selling."

"Well, you should definitely come over. I've been thinking about taking on another assistant."

"I will! That would be so great. What was it you wanted to know? Are you really working on the case?"

"In a very unofficial capacity, if you know what I mean. If Gage comes by again you mustn't say anything about me calling. He gets all strict and spanky if I go behind his back." Landry sucked in a breath, realizing what he'd said.

"You can tell he's a Dom from a mile away," Sorrell said, sounding wistful. "Not that he said anything while he was here, but I did get the feeling that he wouldn't have hesitated to cane my ass if I hadn't answered his questions."

"He does give off that kind of vibe doesn't he?"

"Is he okay by the way? I heard from one of my colleagues that he ran into some trouble."

"Luckily he has a hard head," Landry replied. "He disturbed someone poking around in your storage unit. That's kind of why I'm trying to track down this particular piece of furniture. I don't want his head getting dented again."

"Tell me what it is you're looking for. I can bring up our current stock list on the computer and check it out for you. If anyone asks I can say a client was inquiring."

"Then I'll definitely buy you that coffee when we meet up." Landry described the desk, not mentioning that it had been shipped from overseas.

"That does sound familiar. It's not something we have in the store…"

Landry waited impatiently while Sorrell interrogated the Antiquarium's records. "Anything?"

"Yes!" Sorrell exclaimed. "It took me a while to spot it because it's listed as a nineteenth century reproduction secretaire, but that must be it, right? It came in on a shipment from the UK."

"That's great, we're on the trail. Can you see if it was sold?"

"That's a different file, wait a sec. I don't recall it ever being here in the store but that doesn't mean… Here it is. Ah, that explains why it was never here. It was sold to another dealer. It makes sense because Mr. Penton was real snobbish about selling reproductions. He probably had this buyer in mind when he got hold of the piece. The rest of the shipment was full of real high-end stuff."

"Who bought it, Sorrell?" Landry tried to keep the impatience out of his voice.

"It went from our storage facility to Number 51. There's a name."

"Don't tell me," Landry said, "Sarah-Lu Clancy."

"How did you know that?"

"Is anyone there with you, Sorrell?" Landry asked.

"Yeah, my colleague Chet is upstairs sorting through some paperwork."

"Sarah-Lu Clancy was murdered. Her body was found at the back of another antique store. You need to be careful. I think someone else is trying to track down that particular piece of furniture."

"Oh my God, then you need to take care too."

"I don't think I've got anything to worry about. He's tracking the desk. The people who bought it are loose ends."

"But what if he finds out you're trying to track it down?"

Landry went cold. "I didn't think of that."

"Oh, speak of the devil. Your detective is knocking on the door. He has some gorgeous blond guy with him. Well, he could interrogate me any day."

"All I'm going to say is don't fall for the accent. Let me have your cell number. I'll call you back soon so that we can get together."

Sorrell rattled off the number then disconnected. Landry went for a walk around the store, trying to get his thoughts in order. He was beginning to realize why Gage was being so protective. The arrival of a small stream of customers was a welcome distraction but once they'd gone Landry had nothing else to think about but the case, and the potential danger he'd put himself in. Every creak from the old building made him jump and five minutes before closing he decided to lock up. He was about to turn the sign on the door when someone pushed it open, shoving him backward.

"Oh my goodness, I'm so sorry. I didn't see you there."

"My bad." Landry rubbed his arm where the door handle had banged against it. "I didn't see you either."

"Are you closing? I can come back some other time."

Landry decided he needed to give the guy a break. "I can give you a few minutes, is there anything special you were looking for?"

"Is it okay if I have a quick look around? I'm not sure exactly what I want but I'll know when I see it. Sorry, I must be your most annoying customer ever."

"Not even close," Landry said, smiling. "Feel free to browse and give me a shout if I can help with anything."

"I appreciate it."

Landry retreated to his seat behind the cash desk and glanced through his messages, keeping half an eye on the customer as he came in and out of view, gradually working his way closer to Landry. He was stocky with muddy brown hair and a few wisps of mustache. He was wearing a trilby style hat and kept the brim tilted over his eyes. Landry was starting to feel a little anxious when there was a flash of blue lights and the brief sound of a police siren from outside. He was just about to go to the window to see what was going on when his lone customer gave him a wave from the door. "Thanks so much. I don't want to keep you so I'll come back with my wife so that we can have a better look around. I'd have to run anything I chose past her anyway, you know how it is."

"Sure, no problem." Once the customer had gone, Landry went straight to the door. He locked it, peering through the glass, but the sidewalk outside was empty and there was no sign of the cops. They'd probably been chasing off some poor homeless guy or loitering teenagers. Across the street, the Eastern Emporium's windows glowed golden, and he could see Prisha's father brushing out their porch. Landry grabbed the pole he needed to pull down the security shutters then made his way through the courtyard out to the front of the store. He locked up quickly then retreated inside after giving Prisha's pop a wave.

Once in the safe haven of his apartment, he changed into soft sweats and a warm fleece, made himself a giant mug of hot chocolate then settled on the couch in front of *Golden Girls* reruns. Outside of being with Gage, this was his happy place. All he needed now was for his Dom to come home to him.

Chapter Thirteen

"How about you give me your full attention, Mr. Sweeting." Gage glared. Sorrell hadn't stopped staring at James Ellery since they'd arrived at Penton's Antiquarium. "Or perhaps I should ask Mr. Ellery to step outside."

"No! There's no need for that. Sorry, I'll concentrate, and call me Sorrell. I keep thinking you're talking to my father."

"It's a nice name." Ellery gave him a lazy, wolfish smile. Sorrell blushed and Gage shook his head.

"Did anyone ever tell you that you look like Rupert Penry Jones? He's one of my favorite actors." Sorrell could have been an anime cartoon character his eyes were that wide.

"I'm told the resemblance is uncanny," Ellery drawled.

"Not helping," Gage growled. "Sorrell, this is a murder investigation, and you need to take it seriously."

"Sorry." Sorrell ducked his head, but Gage could see he was still eyeing Ellery through his lashes. Gage moved to block his view. Sorrell was sitting on the edge of the sales desk at the back of the store, legs swinging. Gage angled himself so that he was standing slightly to one side, blocking sight of Ellery who was lounging against the wall. Sorrell's lower lip jutted a little though he hadn't quite made it to a full-blown pout.

"First things first." Gage was impatient to get down to business. "After my last visit, did either of your colleagues leave the premises?"

"Uh, yeah. They both did. They left me here by myself. Chet said he needed some air, which translates as wanting a smoke. He came back later but I can't say how long he was gone because I was upstairs. I didn't see him for at least two hours, but he could have come back into the store before that. Marla went home about ten minutes after your visit. Said she wasn't feeling well, which wasn't surprising considering the amount she'd drunk. She called a cab and left her car here."

"And what about you, Sorrell, did you go anywhere?"

"No. I stayed here and mainlined coffee until I sobered up then I met a friend at Oakley's bookstore. They have a great coffee shop and an amazing second-hand section. Andrea and I meet there about once a month to catch up and buy too many books. She's an old friend from college and works at a bank not too far from here. I can give her your number if you want to check."

"Ellery, go get Chet's story. He's working upstairs." Ellery didn't argue and Gage turned back to Sorrell. "Anything else you'd like to tell me about that day?"

"Only that I heard you ran into some trouble at the storage facility. I hope you weren't hurt."

"Nothing serious. I'm more interested in why someone was in your storage unit in the first place and what they were looking for. What can you tell me about an overseas shipment from the UK that would have arrived about a month ago?"

"What do you need to know? I put the relevant information into a folder after I spoke to Landry."

"I'm sorry, after you spoke to who?" Gage narrowed his eyes and Sorrell gulped.

"I guess I shouldn't have said that. It just slipped out. Oopsie."

"Start from the beginning and tell me exactly what you discussed with my boyfriend. He's not going to be sitting comfortably for a week."

"Landry called earlier. He said he was helping with the case and he wanted to know if there was a particular piece in the shipment. There was. He seemed kind of excited until I told him that we'd had it in storage but then sold it on."

"To Sarah-Lu Clancy at Number 51." Gage sighed.

"That's what he said. Why are you asking me questions if you both already know the answers?"

"That's something I'm wondering about myself." Gage ran a hand through his hair. "Unbelievable. Is there anything you've thought of since you spoke to Landry? Anything you didn't tell him?"

"Actually there is. I was still on the phone to him when you arrived so I didn't get a chance to mention that Sarah-Lu is well known as a flipper."

"I'm guessing you're not talking about dolphins." Gage tapped his foot impatiently.

"No, but dolphins are cute."

"Stick to the subject, please. Enlighten me."

"You heard of flipping houses, right, where somebody buys a property, maybe does a bit of work then sells it really fast with no intention of ever living in it? Well flipping antiques is the same thing. Dealers will buy from other dealers at low rates, knowing they can renovate the piece or they have a buyer waiting in the wings. The item never hits the open market, and the flipper maximizes their profit. Everyone wins because the selling dealer makes more on a quick turnover. Sarah-Lu did that a lot. Number 51 isn't very big and tends to stock ceramics, paintings, glass, that kind of thing, but she flipped a lot of furniture on the side. I wouldn't be surprised if that's what she planned for the piece Landry was interested in—a reproduction secretary desk or secretaire."

"I don't suppose you happen to know where Sarah-Lu stored the items she was going to flip?"

"No, sorry, I don't. She would have arranged her own pickup from our place down by the river, but I never dealt with her direct. The deals were always made between her and Mr. Penton. I guess you could ask Chet, he's more senior than me, so Mr. Penton might have told him more."

"Chet doesn't know either," Ellery said as he reappeared. "I followed the same line of questioning."

Sorrell's entire attention switched to Ellery. "If Sarah-Lu did flip the piece this killer is interested in, then whoever bought it from her is going to be next on his hit list, isn't he?"

"Or she." Gage's frown deepened. "We need to get over to Number 51."

"I doubt there'll be anyone there," Ellery said. "It's getting late and besides, after her death the store is probably closed, especially if it's a smaller business."

"Which could give us a time advantage if we can get hold of someone with access to the books. Let's go. Sorrell, if you think of anything else that might be useful, you have my card."

"Do you have a card, Mr. Ellery?" Sorrell looked way too hopeful.

"No, he doesn't." Gage glared at Ellery until he moved. He hustled him toward the door. "You leave Sorrell alone. He's far too sweet for the likes of you."

"But he's cute and Tad and I have a very open relationship."

"You'd eat him alive. Keep your hands off."

"I have to get my entertainment somewhere. The nights are long and lonely with Tad on the other side of the Atlantic. Of course, if you could see fit to share young Landry for a night, I'm sure we'd have a great deal of fun. On the other hand, perhaps he likes to watch. If you don't want to share him, I'd be more than happy to have you while he watched."

"How is it that you're still alive?" Gage reached the Jeep. He was tempted to drive off and leave Ellery on the sidewalk and he would have if it hadn't been safer to keep Ellery where he could see him.

"Talent, charm and I'm pretty. It helps. I know you're tempted."

"Fuck my life. Get in and put your seatbelt on. I'd hate for you to go through the windshield if I have to stop suddenly."

Gage drove across town faster than he should have. Number 51 wasn't in the city center but a little way out in a small, leafy mall. When they arrived, there were still cars in the lot, but they proved to be there for the several fast-food outlets, which were still open.

Number 51 was closed and there was no sign of life when Gage peered through a slim gap in the shutters.

"It was worth a try," Ellery said.

"I think we're going to have to employ a less targeted approach. We'll run by the precinct, and I'll get someone working on sending out information requests to every dealer in the city. We need to know if anyone bought goods from Sarah-Lu Clancy recently. I know Landry thinks this desk, bureau, whatever it's called, could be the answer but we can't narrow it down that much."

"You know it would be quicker to ask Landry to do it. He's bound to have a contact list. From what we're hearing, these dealers do business with each other all the time. I would guess his boss contacts people about stuff he has for sale and buys from them too."

"That's not a bad idea," Gage said, grudgingly.

"You hate that I had a decent idea, don't you?"

Gage glowered. "It's after seven. Treasure Trove will have closed. I'll give Landry a call now then after we've paid mall security a quick visit to ask them to keep a close eye on Number 51, we'll find somewhere to grab a bite. I'll co-opt someone at the precinct to track down Number 51's employees so we're covering all bases."

"Sounds like a plan. Can we get pancakes? I have an urge."

"I really, *really* don't want to hear about your urges." Despite his words, Gage checked the mall map. The security team were amenable to helping out so Gage headed for IHoP. He sent Ellery inside to grab a table while he called Landry.

"Give him my love," Ellery said, before disappearing inside. Gage counted to ten before making the call.

"Gage! Are you on your way home?"

"Not yet. It'll be a while. We're across town now and about to grab food at the IHoP. Should be back after that though."

"I miss you and I can't believe you're getting pancakes with James instead of me."

"Believe me, neither can I. When I get back we're going to discuss the conversation you had with Sorrell Sweeting at Penton's Antiquarium earlier today."

"Oh, that. Sorrell is a sweetie, isn't he? We're going to meet up for coffee."

"Landry."

"I couldn't help myself. By discuss, do you mean with words, or with your hand against my backside?"

"What do you think? But that can wait. I need you to do something for me." Gage outlined the plan and Landry jumped at the chance to help.

"Of course I can do that. You want me to warn people to be careful?"

"No. I don't want you to refer to the case at all. Can you word it so that it seems like you're looking for a piece for a customer you have lined up?"

"Sure. We mail around all the time if someone comes in asking about something specific that we don't have and we get lots of dealers asking if we have things too. This circulation list gets used a lot, so it won't get spammed."

"Okay, you may redeem yourself a little by getting this done. You have the doors locked, right?"

"Yeah, after I spoke to Sorrell I got a little freaked out."

"Why, did something happen in the store?"

"No, but I gave Petey the afternoon off because Carson went off shift, so I was on my own then some guy barged through the door just as I was closing… He just wanted a look around though. I closed up fine and there was no one else about. I love that you asked though. How's your day been? Have you killed Ellery yet?"

"Frustrating and Ellery is still breathing, though it was a close thing when he suggested a threesome. He also offered to fuck me while you watched if we weren't up for a threesome." Landry went silent. "You're thinking about it, aren't you?"

"Sounds kinda hot."

"Good Lord. Scrub your mind with bleach. We will definitely *not* be talking about this later."

Landry was still giggling as he disconnected. Gage stared at his cell. "Unbelievable." He headed inside the IHoP to find Ellery sitting at a corner table chatting to a server, who was fluttering around him as if he were some kind of movie star.

"I ordered blueberry pancakes. What do you want?" Ellery asked.

"French toast and black coffee." Gage smiled at the server. His dinner companion wasn't her fault, after all.

As she walked away, Gage leaned back in his seat with a groan. "I need a back rub in the worst way."

Ellery grinned. "I should have ordered whipped cream and we could have combined the two. Have you got Landry on the case?"

"You are one sick puppy and yes, I put him to work. Now shut up and let me wallow in self-pity for a while."

Chapter Fourteen

By the end of the following day, Gage was beginning to think that an alternative career might be preferable. Something that didn't involve interaction with anyone.

"Lighthouse keeper."

"Is that the codename for some psycho serial killer, or have you completely lost the plot?" James Ellery sat in Sancha's seat, twisting a pencil between his fingers in a series of rapid, deft movements.

"Why is nothing going our way?" Gage stood then paced up and down. "We've spent all day talking to Sarah-Lu Clancy's family, associates and sales staff and learned precisely zilch. I don't want to speak ill of the dead, but that woman's business practices were shady. Everyone says the same thing. She kept everything in her head. Even her accountant said she'd given him white hairs trying to sort out her tax return every year."

"Sorrell Sweeting was right though. Her colleagues did admit that she flipped bigger pieces all the time. Has Landry come up with anything more useful?"

"He emailed a copy of his contact list, and I've been crossing off the ones that have gotten back to him today to say that they hadn't bought anything from her. He's done surprisingly well with the number of responses. Roughly half the people he sent emails to have replied already. He's forwarding me copies of all the replies, and I have to say there are far too many people in the antiques world that lust after my boyfriend. Three wanted to know if he was free for a date. One wanted to know if he had dumped me yet. I need to lock him up and throw away the fucking key."

"We need a break, and by that, I mean a rest break, not a break in the case. Is a trip to Scorch still on the cards for tonight?"

"I don't recall saying anything about you being invited."

"You mean you would deprive your partner, the man who saved your worthless life, of a little R&R?"

"Emotional blackmail doesn't work when Landry tries it, I'm hardly gonna fall for it from you. You wouldn't know a real emotion if it smacked you in the face."

"Cold."

"If you want a ride back to your hotel you need to stop talking."

"Okay, but seriously, what time are you guys heading out tonight? Is there a dress code? Leather is good, right? I'll even stand a round of drinks."

Exasperated, Gage stood, grabbed his jacket then headed for the door before he did some damage to Ellery's face.

* * * *

146

When he got home, Gage found Landry primping in the bathroom. Music echoed through the apartment, and Landry was shaking his very naked ass as he played with his hair, stopping every now and again to sing into his hairbrush.

"Well, that's a pretty sight." Gage lounged in the doorway.

Landry squeaked and dropped the brush. "Sir! I didn't hear you come in."

"Why am I not surprised? Did you leave me any hot water? I need to wash off the scent of Ellery's cologne. That stuff wafts everywhere. Probably costs five hundred dollars a bottle."

"Partnership still going well then?" Landry unbuttoned Gage's shirt then planted a few kisses on his chest. "You smell fine to me. We're meeting Petey and Carson downstairs in half an hour. What are you going to wear?"

"What would you like me to wear?" Gage kicked off his boots then toed off his socks while Landry got to work on his zipper.

"As little as possible?" Landry said, batting his lashes.

"That's a better look on you, I think."

Landry pouted. "Has to be leather then. The smell of it really turns me on. That older pair of black pants, the ones that are well worn in and cling to your thighs. Damn, now I'm getting hard."

Gage got into the shower then turned on the spray, grateful that Landry had already warmed it up. As he lathered, he watched Landry scrape the peach fuzz from his chin. Gage's own bristles would take a bit more effort. "How about you? Gonna squeeze yourself into some rubber tonight?"

"I think so. Do you have any preferences?"

"The one piece that looks like a short wetsuit."

"The one with the ass cut out?"

Gage cleared his throat. "That's the one." He peeked around the shower door to find Landry blushing and jacking his cock. "What exactly do you think you're doing?"

"All the talcum powder in the world is not going to help me get that outfit on when I'm like this. I'm being practical."

"Oh that's what you call it, is it? Drop it, Landry. I'll deal with that when I'm dry and dressed. Go wait in the bedroom. On your knees."

Landry's eyes widened and he ran his tongue over his lower lip. "Yes, Sir."

Knowing that Landry was waiting gave Gage plenty of motivation to get through his shower quickly. He contemplated shaving but decided to go with stubble, as Landry loved the burn against his skin. He toweled his hair roughly, leaving it tousled and messy, then padded through to the bedroom. Landry was kneeling on the floor in front of the bed, head bowed, hands clasped behind his back. His erection twitched and the head of his cock gleamed with moisture.

Someone is primed and ready. Fuck, he's beautiful.

Gage went to the dresser where he pulled out a slim leather collar and matching set of cuffs. He laid them on the bed next to a slender cane. "Stand up, love. Keep your hands behind your back."

Landry rose in a smooth, graceful movement. Without comment, Gage fastened the collar and cuffs in place then stood back to admire his sub. "That's better. Nobody at Scorch will be in any doubt tonight that you're mine."

Landry whimpered.

"You want to come so bad now, don't you?" Gage reached for Landry's shaft, wrapping it in a loose grip. "My leather around your neck turns you on." Landry gave a jerky nod. His cheeks were flushed, his skin hot. "Turn around, bend over the bed."

Landry spun around so fast he overbalanced. Gage was right there to catch him and hold him until he stabilized. "I've got you." Once he was presented with the perfect view of Landry's smooth backside, Gage picked up the cane. He flexed it then laid a single stripe across Landry's ass, eliciting an indignant yelp. He tossed the cane onto the bed before sinking to his knees. "Keep your hands behind your back. You can come, but no touching." Gage parted Landry's butt cheeks, licked the length of his crack then stuck his tongue into Landry's hole.

Landry wailed and his thighs trembled. Gage rubbed his rough cheeks over Landry's skin as he rimmed him, pushing deep with his tongue, taking in his unique but familiar scent and taste. In seconds Landry came, his body jerking. Gage caught the warm liquid in his palm then held it to Landry's lips. Landry lapped as his body continued to spasm. Surging to his feet in time to support Landry's trembling frame, Gage pushed his rigid dick against Landry's damp hole. He didn't attempt penetration, but rubbed himself to fulfillment, the stream of his cum sliding down Landry's thighs. Landry turned into his arms, eyes glazed and expression dreamy.

"Not a bad way to start the evening," Gage commented.

"Not bad at all, Sir. You turned me to Jell-O."

Gage guided Landry to the bed. "Sit. Take a breath. I'll fetch a washcloth because there's no time for more showers."

After a quick clean-up and a lot of cajoling, Gage managed to get himself and Landry dressed and out the door only five minutes later than planned. They found Carson and Petey waiting at the bottom of the stairs.

"Oh wow! Someone looks well fucked." Petey hip checked Landry.

Landry grinned. He had on loose sweats and a coat over his outfit and had chosen black tennis shoes for footwear. "I so am." He linked arms with Petey and the two of them headed for the street talking a mile a minute.

"How many hours have they been apart?" Carson asked.

Gage shook his head as he locked up behind them. "Those two can talk for weeks about absolutely nothing. Half an hour ago, Landry was barely coherent. I need to up my game if he can recover this quickly."

Carson chuckled. "It's good to be going somewhere. It's been too long since we hung out at the club."

"I definitely need to decompress. The case I'm working on makes my head hurt."

"Are you sure that's not your partner?"

"I miss Sancha. I'm not tempted to shoot her nearly so often as I am James-fucking-Ellery. Christ, that man gives Brits a bad name."

Gage put all thoughts of Ellery out of his head while he drove to Scorch. Petey and Landry were chattering nonstop in the back and half the time, Gage had no idea who or what they were talking about. He shot Carson a questioning glance.

"Don't ask me." Carson shrugged. "I caught naked water polo, opalescent nail polish and black carrots—in one sentence."

"There are black carrots?"

"Apparently."

Parking slots near Scorch were nonexistent, so Gage dropped everyone at the door while he drove a couple blocks to the nearest lot. There was no line to join when he got back, so he flashed his membership card, checked his jacket then strolled across the club to the area set aside for comfortable seating. It was far enough away from the dance floor that it was possible to hold a conversation without yelling. Elsewhere the music pounded—something Gage could only tolerate for short periods.

Carson's height made him easy to spot. He'd snagged a corner table and a server was hovering when Gage reached the group.

"What the actual fuck on a stick?" Gage glared. James Ellery sat on one end of a squishy, black velvet couch, his arm around Sorrel Sweeting.

"Hey, partner. Thought you'd be wearing a chauffeur cap or a valet uniform. Loving the leather trousers though. Very snug."

Carson stepped in front of Gage. "If you hit him, you'll have to arrest yourself."

"Iced water with a slice of lime, please." Gage got the words out between gritted teeth. The server, eyes wide, scurried away.

"Sir! Isn't it great? James brought Sorrel with him. It's his first time at Scorch. This is so much more fun than meeting over coffee—though we are gonna do that too, because cake cannot be missed. Why don't they serve cake here? They so should."

Landry got up to grab Gage's hand then pulled him toward a couch. Gage caught Ellery's sly grin.

"Landry, uh, there seems to be a bit of your pants missing." Sorrel was the color of a ripe tomato.

"I know! Aren't they fabulous?"

"I think you sat on a crease or something. There's a red line across your butt."

"A cane will do that." Landry giggled.

"Sit." Gage turned Landry around so that Ellery couldn't see his ass then pulled him onto his lap. He checked the fit of Landry's collar and Landry placed his smaller hand over Gage's.

"I love you, remember?"

"I know. I think it's time we made this permanent, don't you?"

Landry gaped. "You mean it?"

"When do I ever say anything I don't mean?" To Gage's dismay, Landry burst into tears. "Hey now, I didn't mean to upset you. If it's not something you want yet, that's fine."

"Of course I want it! I'm crying because I'm happy. *So* happy." Landry sobbed anew, burying his face against Gage's shoulder, soaking his T-shirt.

Gage stroked Landry's hair. "We'll talk about what kind of collar you want. My leather looks good around your neck though."

"I want what you want, of course."

"I want everyone to know you're mine."

"Especially James?" Landry said, scrubbing the tears from his face with a smile.

"God yes."

"You have nothing to worry about, you know? He's not my type. I prefer tall, dark and grumpy."

"Good to know." Gage glowed inside. He wanted to shout to the world that Landry was all his. He caught Carson's eye and got a thumbs-up. Petey had a soppy grin on his face and even Ellery was beaming. "I guess you all heard that?"

"Seems like tonight has turned into a celebration," Carson said.

Landry jiggled in Gage's lap. "We should order celebratory snacks. Loaded nachos all around?"

Their server arrived with a tray of drinks and Ellery put in the food order. Landry clapped his hands together in glee. "Best night ever. Petey, if you're going to try out the new wheel maybe you should do that before you eat something. It's gonna be spinny." He whirled a finger in the air.

"Landry has a good point, love." Carson gave Petey's shoulder a squeeze. "I know you're excited to give it a go."

"I want to. We can order more food later, can't we?"

"Of course we can. Why don't we go check out the wheel?"

Petey got to his feet.

"Are you guys talking about a roulette wheel or something? Is there gambling here?" Sorrel asked.

"It's not that kind of wheel," Landry said, giggling. "Look over there on the stage."

Sorrell stood to get a better view. On the stage at the back of the dancefloor, the huge bondage wheel was being maneuvered into place. A small crowd was gathering to watch.

"It's going to be popular," Petey said. "We may not get a turn."

"I don't think we need to worry about that," Carson said as one of the Dungeon Masters approached the group.

"Hey Gage, Carson... We are about ready for you."

Carson nodded. "On our way."

"Excellent. The stage is yours as soon as you're ready."

"What's going on?" Petey asked.

"Well, I called ahead and offered to do a demonstration," Carson said. "You okay with that?"

"Yes!" Petey scrambled to his feet, narrowly avoiding knocking over all their drinks in his excitement.

"That's what I thought." Carson took his hand then tugged him toward the stage.

"You're so good to me, Sir."

"You don't mind if we don't sign up for that, do you?" Landry asked.

"Considering you told me you got sick on '*It's a Small World*' at Disneyland, I'm guessing this is on the red list as far as we're concerned," Gage said.

"I'd eaten too much cotton candy, and this isn't the same. People are not designed to be upside down," Landry muttered.

"Is that what happens?" Sorrell asked, rising on his toes so he could get a better view.

"Carson is going to strap Petey to the wheel, so he's bound and helpless. He'll spin him upside down then flog him until he screams. Then I'd guess he'll fuck him until he screams some more," Ellery said.

"Oh my." Sorrell's pants were tented.

"How about you and I go stand near the front so you can watch?" Ellery got to his feet.

"Can we?"

"Yes we can. Carson wouldn't have put them both forward to demonstrate if he wasn't up for having Petey on display. I'm guessing that once they get started, Petey will be oblivious to anything but Carson."

They moved away, leaving Landry and Gage to guard their drinks and couches.

"I think Sorrell might be discovering some interests he didn't know he had," Landry said.

"And I think you should focus on me." Gage dug in his pocket, pulling out a sachet of lube. "Talking about collaring you permanently has gotten me hard. I think you should do something about that, don't you?"

Landry beamed. He straddled Gage's thighs. "Did I mention how much I love these pants?"

"Once or twice," Gage said, sucking in a breath as Landry petted his leather-clad thigh, before lowering his zipper to release Gage's straining cock.

"Oh, someone's perky!"

"*Perky*...I will gag you, brat."

"Yes, Sir." Landry gave Gage's cock a few deft strokes and Gage's ability to think narrowed to a single topic. He handed the lube to Landry who tugged at the slippery plastic packet until it split apart, splattering his hands with the clear, glistening substance. "Oopsie."

"Put that where you need to. You, me... Don't care, just be quick."

Landry lubed Gage's cock then positioned himself above it. Gage had enough presence of mind to grab his arm. "Are you sure you're ready? I don't want you hurting yourself."

"As ready as you are." After one slippery false start and a lot of giggling, Landry connected his hole with

Gage's dick then sank into his lap, lips parted and eyes wide.

"Fuck!" Gage grabbed Landry's hips.

"Yes please!" Landry writhed in place, squeezing his inner muscles to compress Gage's shaft. His muscles rippled as he undulated to his own rhythm. He sank his teeth into his lower lip, his expression intense with concentration.

Christ on a stick, this is going to be embarrassingly fast. Gage thrust to meet Landry's movements. He managed to stay coordinated for a while, but it proved impossible to maintain control for long. He shifted position to drive deeper into Landry's body then growled as his orgasm rolled through him.

"Please, Sir!"

Gage could only manage a brief nod to let Landry know he had permission to come. Landry had to unzip the front of his outfit from chest to groin before he could release his cock. He cursed, fingers fumbling but finally managed to grip his shaft and tugged himself to completion. Sated, he collapsed against Gage's chest.

"So good, Sir, but whose idea was it for me to wear this getup?"

"I like it just fine, nice and accessible for me."

"Whereas for me, not so much."

"It was amusing, watching you struggle."

"So mean!"

"Not denying it. We should clean up before the others get back. I'm not averse to an audience but on this occasion, I'm glad Carson and Petey provided a distraction. James Ellery is enough to deflate anyone's erection."

Landry wriggled free of Gage's softened cock and made a grab for a napkin. He gave them both a cursory cleanup before zipping Gage's fly then assuming a far more demure position. "Ooh nachos!" Their server placed two huge dishes on the table. "We don't have to wait for the others, do we?"

Gage pulled one of the dishes closer. "You snooze, you lose. Feed me, slave boy."

"Whatever my master desires." Landry batted his lashes.

"I desire you to cover up before the others get back." Gage dealt with Landry's zipper.

Landry gave him a questioning look. "Really? You know my ass is hanging out of this suit, don't you?"

"But your ass has my mark on it. Something I think should be a permanent thing. Gonna get you tattooed along with that collar."

Landry massaged his rubber-covered package. "Shouldn't have worn something so tight, dammit."

"I'm thinking a little pair of handcuffs and my initials. Maybe a guiche too."

"Oh!" Landry squirmed, making Gage grin.

Gage grabbed a loaded nacho then crunched happily. "Gonna run a chain from the guiche to a butt plug then order you to keep still. One stroke of the cane for every twitch."

Landry moaned. "Sir, stop!"

"Stop what?" Gage handed the nacho plate to Landry. "Your service needs improving."

"You are way too pleased with yourself right now." Landry fed Gage a steady series of sour cream and salsa loaded chips.

Gage smacked his lips. "Life is good. One night of peaceful kink is exactly what I need."

"Now you're tempting fate. The others are coming back."

Soon their table was crowded once again. Gage basked in the knowledge that Landry wanted to be his just as much as Gage wanted to mark his ownership. Even James Ellery couldn't put a damper on his mood.

Chapter Fifteen

A little while later, Landry slipped away to the bathroom to check his cell. He didn't want to miss a message from someone in possession of the secretaire. He leaned against the hand basin enjoying the feel of cool porcelain against his still warm butt and scrolled through his emails. Most of his contacts were just saying hi, asking when he could meet up, or if Treasure Trove had anything that might be of interest but then he froze. He read the message again.

"No, no, no! That can't be right. How do I not know about this?" He barged past two guys kissing in a corner before tearing across the club. "Gage!" Gage was on his feet as he arrived, looking around for danger.

"What? I knew I should have gone to the can with you. Did someone hurt you?"

"No, nothing like that. Sit down so the others can hear." Once Landry had his audience, he took a breath. "I found out who has the piece of furniture we've been chasing. We do!"

"What do you mean 'we'?" Gage said, taking Landry's cell from his outstretched hand.

"It has to be the most traveled antique in Seattle. It turns out that Sarah-Lu Clancy at Number 51 flipped it to Josephine Mackay, but her manager didn't keep it. He handed it off in a truckload of stuff that Mr. Lao bought."

"Oh my God." Petey went white, jerked out of sub space as if he'd been attached to an elastic band that had snapped. Carson gathered him into a hug.

"Why didn't you know about this?" Ellery asked.

"Mr. Lao still does most of the buying for Treasure Trove. He and I discuss stock rotation and what's coming into the store, but I don't always know what his most recent purchases are."

Ellery frowned. "And I guess you have some kind of storage facility? That stockroom you have at the back of the store is way too small to keep furniture."

"I should have fucking checked there first," Gage muttered. "Regardless of the trail. Treasure Trove has half of the warehouse at the back of the Eastern Emporium across the street."

Landry nodded. "That's right." He explained for James' benefit. "Prisha's dad lets us have the space he doesn't need for next to nothing. In exchange he uses some of our pieces in his window displays and we send customers his way for antique rugs and carpets, which he imports from places like Turkey and Morocco."

"The latest body was dumped at the back of Josephine's. That could be a coincidence, but I doubt it," Ellery said.

"I think it may be," Gage suggested. "Remember, the first body was found outside Treasure Trove. This killer is sending a message to Seattle's antique trade that they aren't safe. He wants an atmosphere of fear but he's a step behind. If he knows now who Sarah-Lu flipped the piece to, then the proprietor of Josephine's is in danger."

"And so is Mr. Lao!" Landry cried.

"Okay, here's what we'll do." Gage took charge. "If it's okay with you, Carson, you take the boys back home and stay with them. Ellery, you and I will track down whoever owns Josephine's and hope we beat the killer to it. Landry, call Mr. Lao and tell him to get somewhere safe."

"Okay...Sir!" Landry needed Gage's arms around him.

"It's going to be okay, love. Your email campaign has hopefully given us an advantage."

"Shouldn't you go find Mr. Lao first?"

"I doubt the killer knows that the piece moved on straight away, and whoever this is is clearing up every loose end. Everyone who's touched that piece of furniture is ending up dead. We have to try to stop another murder and the victim is more likely to be someone from Josephine's than Mr. Lao."

"What about me?" Sorrell whispered.

"Carson will take you with the boys too," Gage said. "I don't think you should be on your own tonight either. You should call your colleagues and let them know what's going on."

Sorrell nodded. He looked scared and Landry leaned across to pat his knee. "Try not to worry. Gage is really good at this stuff and James is champion sneaky. They'll get this done."

"Are you sure you don't need me to help in some way?" Carson asked.

"Keeping the boys safe is the most important thing you could be doing right now," Gage said. "I wouldn't trust anyone else with Landry. Now, we need to get going. Ellery and I will go as we are. I'll take the Jeep. Carson, you call a cab. The boys need to put more clothes on before you leave, and we can't wait."

Gage gave Landry a quick kiss before he and Ellery headed for the exit. Landry looked around at his shell-shocked friends. "Life around me can get interesting, can't it?"

Carson rolled his eyes. "Interesting is one way of putting it. Come on, you guys go get changed into street clothes while I sort out a cab."

"He's going to be okay, isn't he?" Landry's fingers strayed to his collar.

"Of course he is. Ellery will annoy any bad guys to death before anything happens to Gage, you can rely on that." Carson gave Landry's shoulder a squeeze. "Gage is a big boy, he can look after himself."

"That's a matter of opinion," Landry muttered, thinking how Gage couldn't even sort laundry without putting one of Landry's bright red thongs in with the white sheets. However, for now he had no choice but to follow Gage's instructions and he'd much rather be at home than sitting at Scorch surrounded by people enjoying themselves in blissful ignorance.

* * * *

By the time Carson, Petey, Landry and Sorrell piled into Petey's tiny apartment, it was after midnight. Sorrell had called both his colleagues from the cab whilst Landry had only managed to reach Mr. Lao's voicemail. He'd left three increasingly panicked messages.

"It's so late. He's probably asleep." Landry threw himself onto the beanbag next to Petey's couch.

"Who wants coffee?" Carson asked, brandishing the pot. "Tea for you, Petey, right?"

"Please. I'll help. Landry will have coffee because…it's coffee and he's Landry. How about you, Sorrell?"

"Yes, please. You have a cute place here, Petey. I share with a bunch of wannabe frat boys and there are things growing in the kitchen that should be donated to science. I'd love a place of my own."

"I used to live here," Landry said, glad to have something normal to talk about. "Mr. Lao had the bigger place downstairs but then he moved in with his girlfriend and made me store manager, so I got the bigger apartment. Petey moved in here when I got to take on an assistant."

"I used to be a cycle courier," Petey piped up, "but then there was this whole thing with diamonds and a hunt for hidden treasure. Long story short, I ended up living here and working at Treasure Trove, then Carson asked me out."

"And this was all after I met Gage and got caught up with the Yakuza and a missing necklace," Landry added.

"You guys sure live exciting lives," Sorrell said. "My idea of a good time is scoring the last slice of peach pie at the diner near home."

"We didn't deliberately get involved in any of this stuff." Landry stared at a moth battering itself against the window. "Trouble seems to hunt me down but it's definitely not my fault."

"You have a whole family here though. I'm a bit jealous." Sorrell nibbled his lower lip.

"Well, you're here and caught up in the mayhem, so that makes you part of the family now." Landry hauled himself out of the beanbag. "Carson, you mind if I go downstairs and put something warmer on? I'll come right back."

Carson poked his head out of the kitchen. "Sure. You can't get into much trouble down one flight of stairs." He paused. "Wait, what am I saying? Of course you can. You have five minutes, Landry. I value my balls and Gage will do bad things to them if anything happens to you. Don't so much as get a splinter, okay?"

"Promise."

For once, Landry did as he was told. He had something in mind, but it would have to wait until Carson wasn't being so watchful. In the meantime, he needed a few things from his apartment including a change of clothes.

Not a lie at all. Crisis situations need snuggly sweaters and comfortable underwear, not assless rubber under baggy sweats.

Being back at home put Gage front and center in Landry's mind. All the worry he'd managed to put aside in the journey from the club came tumbling back. Landry sniffed and rubbed at his eyes with the back of his hand. "Not crying. It's late and I'm tired is all." He went to the closet and pulled out one of Gage's thick sweaters. After stripping off completely, he dressed from the bottom-up in a sensible pair of shorts, T-shirt and jeans. Gage's sweater went over the top, the sleeves rolled three times. Woolly socks and an old pair of shoes completed the outfit. Landry also grabbed a backpack, filling it with a few things he thought he might find useful later. He left the apartment and went back upstairs. He tucked the bag behind a potted plant on the landing before going into Petey's place.

Carson had produced drinks and a plate of cookies, which were on the table in front of Sorrell. Petey was in Carson's lap on the couch with Sorrell in the single armchair. Landry returned to his beanbag and reached for his coffee.

"That's so much better. Much as I love rubber, it's a little…clingy."

Sorrell snorted. "Your ass was hanging out."

"I had sweats on over the top," Landry protested. "I was decent."

"I'd never be brave enough to wear something like that."

"Why not? You stick out more at Scorch the more you wear, especially if you are a sub. Doms are okay, they can wear an entire cow and nobody bats an eyelid."

"There was a lot of skin on view. Is that why they keep it so warm in there?"

"I've never really thought about it," Landry admitted. "The temperature isn't generally top of my mind when I'm in there. Did you have a good time? Even though the night was a bit shorter than it should have been."

"I did. I was kind of nervous but it was fun. Everyone seemed to be having such a good time. I'm not saying that I'd want to be strapped to that wheel and flogged any time soon…"

"You'd love it," Petey interjected. "You've no idea how wonderful it is to feel your skin warm under an expertly wielded flogger. Being spun round and turned upside down makes it even more special."

"Don't listen to him," Landry said. "Some of us like to spend our nights out the right way up. Floggers, however… Can't argue with that. I have to say though, Sorrell, you do know that James has a boyfriend?"

"Of course. I Skyped with Tad after James asked me to go to Scorch with him. James told me he had a partner who was over in England but that they had a relaxed relationship and that Tad wouldn't mind at all if we spent the evening together. I said to Tad that James said the two of them had, in his words, a very open relationship, and Tad said he was lying. Well, not lying. He was trying to take the piss. He said their relationship is anything but open. James calls him every night and makes him…um…while he watches."

Landry snickered. "He does, does he?"

"The man is totally besotted with Tad and Tad is with him, but he didn't mind him being my friend and having a fun night. Tad is so pretty. He and James together must be a stunning couple."

Landry gaped. "I had no idea that James had even an ounce of integrity in his body."

"He was a complete gentleman. He's so good-looking—I knew he couldn't possibly be single. It was really kind of him to invite me along."

"Landry and James have history," Petey commented.

"Oh, I know." Sorrell sounded delighted. "James made your adventures sound so much fun. Did you know he travels all over the world for his job?"

Landry counted to ten beneath his breath. "He mentioned it, yes."

Petey snickered, burying his face against Carson's chest. Sorrell smothered a yawn. "Sorry, I'm not used to being up this late without a lot of caffeine. I can be online with my gaming buddies until the early hours, no problem, but I chain-drink Red Bull to keep me going. I'm flagging without my fix."

"I'm not much of a night owl either," Landry admitted. "Must be getting old."

"When you came back from the stage earlier, Petey, you were all dreamy and looked so happy." Sorrell frowned. "Is that what's called sub space?"

"That's right," Petey confirmed. "It doesn't happen to everyone, and the triggers are different, but Carson always takes me to my happy place. I kind of drift away, detached from anything except sensation and the connection between me and Carson. It's wonderful."

"That sounds amazing."

"It is but I came down with a bit of a crash. Aftercare is important. Carson always makes sure I'm okay."

"It's a Dom's responsibility to look after his sub," Carson growled, pulling Petey closer. Petey gave a happy sigh.

"I'm jealous," Sorrell admitted. "I'll admit I've no idea if BDSM is my thing, but I'm curious. How do you guys deal with your men being first responders? Aren't you scared?"

"I always worry when Carson is on a shift, especially if there's a big fire on the news, but he's great at his job and he loves it," Petey said.

"I worry too," Landry admitted, "but I'd never try to guilt Gage out of the job. It's part of who he is. He was a detective before he met me."

"And uniforms are hot, right?" Sorrell grinned.

"Gage doesn't get his dress uniform out very often, but he does like using his handcuffs," Landry said, straight-faced. "A lot. I wish I knew where he was right now." He reached for his phone and tried Mr. Lao's number again. "Still no reply from Mr. Lao." He texted Gage to let him know he hadn't been able to get hold of his boss.

"He's not defenseless," Petey said. "Remember when he tackled those Yakuza goons?"

"True. I think he's forgotten more about martial arts than I'll ever know." Landry grinned. "Talk about never judging a book by its cover." He yawned, setting everyone else off again. "I think I'm gonna try to take a nap. There's more room downstairs, Carson. Shall we relocate? You and Petey can have the spare room and Sorrell can take the couch."

"Sounds like a plan," Carson said. "I think we should all stay together."

After Carson and Petey grabbed some toiletries, including a spare toothbrush for Sorrell, they all trooped downstairs to Landry and Gage's larger apartment. Landry left the others to take turns in the bathroom and went to his room. He took off his shoes but climbed under the covers fully dressed, pulling them up to his neck. Carson leaned in to say goodnight. He left the door open a crack, and Landry listened to the creaking floorboards as the others settled in for the night.

Too nervous to sleep, Landry amused himself imagining role-play scenarios with Gage. He thought Gage would make a good strict professor to his tardy student, or a pirate captain to his cabin boy. He could definitely imagine Gage in a frilly shirt, open to the navel, skull and crossbones tattooed on his bicep. Landry's cock thought it was a great plan too and began to harden.

No, down boy. This is not a good time.

Landry let his mind stray to Gage and James, somewhere out in the city tracking a killer in the middle of the night. It worked and his erection subsided. He mulled over Sorrell's question about what it was like to have a detective as a partner. Most of the time it was something he could compartmentalize in the back of his mind. Gage and Sancha looked out for each other but Landry still worried. He hated guns, but they were unavoidable in Gage's line of work. He'd already had some close shaves and Landry could do without that ever happening again.

He better be wearing his vest. If I find out he's gone out without it, I'll shoot him myself. Then I'll tell Sancha when she gets back, and she'll shoot him too. Why is it when I want time to pass quickly, it moves slower than Gage when I ask him to do the dishes?

Landry sighed. When the glowing clock on his phone hit two-thirty, he threw the covers back. He slipped his keys into his pocket, picked up his shoes then crept to the door. He froze, listening for a full minute for any sign that anyone else in the apartment was awake. Light snoring came from the spare room though he couldn't tell whether it was Petey or Carson. There was no sign of life from the living room where Sorrell was nesting in a cocoon of blankets on the couch.

Holding his breath, Landry pushed open his bedroom door. Avoiding the creaky board in the hall, he made it to the apartment's front door in silence. The next part of his plan was much harder. There was a slight click when he disengaged the latch and he stilled again, listening hard. The door handle was quite stiff and Landry decided that speed was safer than caution. He depressed the handle and pulled the door in one swift motion. The hinges were well greased and silent. He stepped out into the hallway then closed the door. Realizing he had been holding his breath, he let it out slowly, afraid that even that would be enough sound to alert Carson if not the others. He held still, head cocked to one side. The occasional vehicle passing outside created a low hum and a slight draft moved a leaf on the plant he'd concealed his bag behind.

Two minutes passed, then he shouldered the bag before padding down the stairs in his socked feet. He sat on the bottom step to put on his runners then unlocked the courtyard door. This one was much heavier, and it was impossible to be completely silent, but Landry hoped that being a floor away from his friends would be enough distance for him to make his escape without being caught.

Once outside, he relaxed a little. He still took care crossing the courtyard, not wanting to kick over a flowerpot by accident and ruin his whole plan after he'd come so far. The gate to the side alley was easy. Gage had oiled the hinges not that long ago because he'd gotten sick of the scraping noise they made, which he said was worse than nails down a chalkboard. Landry left the access points unlocked so that he had an easy route home. He didn't intend to be long. He stopped to pull a dark hat and gloves from his backpack. His blond hair stood out too much, and he didn't want to touch anything he found with bare hands. He'd also stashed a tin of Gage's boot polish and smeared some of it on his cheeks.

Suitably ninjafied, he paused at the end of the alley. He watched a cab approach then pass. A rat scurried along the gutter before disappearing into a drain. The air smelled faintly of gas and exhaust fumes. When it was clear, Landry ran across the street then down the side of the Eastern Emporium. There were movement-activated security lights in the rear parking lot, so Landry skirted the edge so that they didn't come on. Prisha's room was at the back of the building, and he didn't want to risk waking her. She'd want to come with him and there was no way he would put her in danger.

The building that Prisha's pop used for storing his stock had a huge roller door at the front which trucks could reverse up to, but Landry made his way down the narrow path skirting the side of the building to another door at the rear. It wasn't often used because Prisha and her dad generally moved stock through the front. It took Landry three attempts to get the key to turn in the lock because it was stiff and a bit rusted. The building had no windows, so once inside, Landry decided it would be safe to use the flashlight app on his phone. He clambered past boxes of the Emporium's stock—rolled-up carpets, piles of rugs and randomly, a giant stoneware elephant.

Treasure Trove's stock was stored down the far side of the building, each piece of furniture covered with a dust cloth. Landry stashed his bag to one side then had to lift each cloth in turn to check what was underneath. Some pieces he recognized and had helped to carry in, but others were unfamiliar. He'd looked through about two thirds of the contents when he found what he was looking for.

"Yes!" He clamped his lips shut, containing his excitement. Folding back the cloth, he exposed what proved to be a beautiful inlaid secretaire with multiple drawers and a pulldown front that formed the desk. Being thorough, he checked all the obvious compartments first but other than a torn shipping label and a dead moth, there was nothing.

"It was never going to be that easy," Landry muttered. He laced his fingers together then flexed them, making his knuckles crack. It was time to find whatever secrets the desk's creator had concealed.

Chapter Sixteen

Landry decided to start at the bottom and work his way up systematically rather than randomly prod at things. First, he felt around each foot, searching for any knobs or depressions that seemed out of place. He also tried twisting but as nothing moved, he concluded the feet were a dead end. He traced the inlay on the cupboard doors, which formed the bottom section of the desk, admiring the intricate design of flowers and leaves. The inlay was a mixture of shell and colored woods. "It's a good thing Mr. Lao didn't move this piece into the store yet, because it would have sold superfast," Landry murmured.

The key to the door was in the lock, which was edged in brass. He opened the door and inside was a shelf dividing the space into two. The bottom was open whilst four dividers separated the top. Landry stuck his arm into each one, feeling right to the back. He jiggled the dividers and felt beneath the shelf. When he knocked at the bottom, there was no indication of any hollow spaces. Disappointed, he dropped to his knees and after locking the cupboard doors again, pulled out the drawer above them. He removed it completely, putting it to one side so that he could reach into the opening and feel around. He drew a blank so examined the drawer, which was lined with dark green velvet. He could see straight away that the side wall of the drawer was thicker on one side than the other. After a bit of fiddling, a false wall section slid free.

"Wow! This is so cool." The space he'd found was only big enough to hold something small, perhaps a pen or a few coins, but it was empty. Landry put everything back as it was, sliding the drawer into place. "Okay, next."

When he pulled down the front part of the desk, two battens on either side of the drawer protruded to take its weight. It was a remarkable piece of craftsmanship. The writing surface was set with a piece of green leather, hand tooled in gold. It bore the indentations of decades of use and what Landry guessed might be a wine stain in one corner. He liked that it wasn't perfect — it gave the piece character. Set to the rear were a series of drawers and cubbies. A false panel revealed an empty cavity but inside was a lever and this released a drawer within a drawer. When Landry felt inside, he found a velvet pouch.

"Oh my God, I was right!" After getting to his feet, Landry loosened the drawstring on the pouch then tipped its contents onto the desk. In front of him lay an exquisite bottle, which he thought might once have contained expensive perfume. The glass was wrapped in a gold metal casing, intricately wrought in a pattern of twisting stems and leaves. There was a gold collar around the neck and a delicate stopper fit snugly in the top.

Landry was admiring the bottle when he thought he heard a creak. Heart pounding, he slipped it back into its pouch then searched for a place to hide it. Once the bottle was concealed, he set about putting the secretaire back together, but his fingers were clumsy with nerves. A fragment of luggage label drifted to the floor, but he ignored it, tugging the dustsheet back over the desk.

Someone was definitely coming into the building. There was a rasp from the door hinge then a light footstep. Frantic, Landry lifted the lid of a heavy trunk then scrambled inside. As he closed the lid, he hoped fervently that the trunk wasn't airtight. He could no longer hear anything and froze in place, hardly daring to breathe. Without warning, the lid crashed open, and Landry was hauled out by his hair before being thrown to the floor.

"Hiding only works when you take your baggage with you." Landry caught his backpack as it was kicked at him. "Get up." Landry got up to face his assailant who was dressed in black and wearing a balaclava. "Did you find what you were looking for?"

"I don't know what you're talking about."

"Yes, you do. Don't play stupid games with me. I've killed a lot of people to get this far, so unless you want to be next, you'll give me what I want."

Landry assessed his options, none of which seemed beneficial to his health. He could try to run, but there were a lot of obstacles in his way, and he didn't find the consequences of being caught appealing. He ruled out fighting. Balaclava man was bigger than him, thickset and scary. He wondered if crying might work.

"You've got ten seconds before I break something and I'm not talking about furniture. A finger to start with, then an arm."

Landry gulped. "Fine. I was looking for a particular piece of furniture and I found it. It's behind you under the cloth."

"The secretary desk I've been chasing all over the fucking city. Don't antique dealers here ever sell anything to the public?" Balaclava man ripped the cloth off the desk. "Finally. You've saved me the trouble of searching it, I hope."

"There's nothing in it."

"I'll be checking that for myself. Open all the drawers and cupboards."

Shaking, Landry did as he was told then stepped to one side. "And the rest. Don't pretend to be stupid. I know who you are."

"How?"

"I was watching when you found the body on your doorstep. That was entertaining. If only I'd known how close this desk was. I could have saved myself a lot of aggravation coming straight here rather than leaving my little warning to the city's antique trade."

"You didn't have to kill Arthur Penton. He didn't know the desk was connected to a suspicious death in England."

"He was a nasty, greedy man. Ending him was a public service. Interesting that you worked out the UK connection—or was that your detective boyfriend? He didn't seem that bright."

Landry triggered the secret mechanisms, revealing all the compartments he'd found. "How did you know the desk was here?"

"A dumb kid I know told me. Thought he was doing me a favor and he was, just not in the way he assumed." Cogs began whirring in Landry's head. Everything was becoming clear. "These are all empty."

"I told you there was nothing there."

"Where's the poison bottle, you little shit?"

"What...?" Landry didn't duck fast enough and a fist connected with his face. His vision blurred.

"I'm going to enjoy taking you apart."

Landry dropped to the floor and curled into a ball, making himself as small as possible. He braced for a blow or kick.

"Fuck, someone's coming."

The killer grabbed Landry's collar, hauled him to his feet then backhanded him. The force sent him tumbling into the same chest he'd hidden in earlier. Pain brought Landry close to vomiting. He looked on in horror as Carson picked his way across the floor.

"Carson, look out!" A dark figure stepped into Carson's path, swung something at his head, which connected with a thud. Carson crumpled to the ground and lay there, unmoving. "You bastard!" Landry rolled out of the trunk. He scrabbled on the floor for the section of luggage label then snatched a pen from the side pocket of his backpack. He only had time to write two letters while balaclava man dragged Carson's body across the floor. Landry staggered to his feet, fell into the side of the secretaire and slipped the paper fragment into one of the secret compartments, which he elbowed shut.

"You and I are going to go somewhere private for a chat." The killer kicked Landry's backpack into a corner then grabbed his arm, twisting it behind his back. He propelled him through the warehouse, banging into things as he went, then outside, cursing the stiff door. Landry had no idea what time it was, but the sun was beginning to rise because it was no longer full dark.

"No way can I trust you to keep quiet."

Landry fought as a piece of cloth was stuffed in his mouth then bound in place with some kind of strap, which cut into the corners of his mouth. Then he was hustled roughly to the street where the killer had a vehicle waiting. He popped the trunk then bundled Landry inside, taking the time to tie Landry's hands behind his back with a towrope before slamming the hood closed. Seconds later the engine started and the car began to move.

The trunk was hot, claustrophobic and smelled of old sweat socks. Landry wriggled into the least uncomfortable position he could manage in the restricted space. His face hurt and one side of his lip had swollen. He tongued it and winced. Otherwise, he seemed to have gotten away with a few bruises.

Gage is not gonna be happy with me. He's never gonna let me out again. Also, he could teach this idiot a thing or two about knots. Landry worked the rope around his wrists and got free in about three minutes. He yanked out the gag.

"Bleh. Gross. I'm gonna need shots after having that in my mouth." A fingertip search of the trunk revealed nothing of use, so Landry looked for a release catch. As a kid, his dad had taught him that all American-made cars had interior safety mechanisms allowing the trunk to be opened from the inside. With two older brothers, Landry was grateful for the knowledge and though they'd never gotten around to locking him in the trunk, he'd never forgotten. He wasn't a car expert, but he thought this one was a Lexus — surely, the same rule would apply to Japanese models too. Sure enough, when he twisted around, he could see the faint, luminescent glow of the catch.

Landry debated his chances. If he popped the catch and threw himself out when the car was going too fast, he'd die. If he landed in the path of another vehicle, he'd be squished. He could wait for the car to slow down or idle at a stop light but if there was no one around, the killer might come after him. He could have a gun and shoot Landry before he could run away.

Think. Think, Landry. What would Gage do?

"Gage wouldn't have gotten himself into this mess in the first place." Landry fought back a sob. His fear was mixed with righteous anger. How dare this asshole think he could go around killing people with impunity?

The sun had been coming up when they'd left the Eastern Emporium. At the time of year that meant it should be approaching five in the morning and by now someone must have gone looking for Carson and also realized that Landry was missing. Unfortunately, Landry didn't think he had time to wait for the cavalry to arrive.

* * * *

"Well, this is cozy," Ellery said, holding tight to the 'oh shit!' handle as Gage drove at high speed through the Seattle streets. "I'd prefer a slower pace for our alone time, but it's dark, it's a nice night... I'm detecting romantic overtones."

"You couldn't detect shit," Gage muttered as he burned rubber turning a corner. "And this doesn't even come close to being a romantic situation. I worry about the way your mind works."

"There are advantages to thinking in curves rather than straight lines, Gage. Gives me the jump on most average humans."

Gage swerved to avoid a trashcan rolling across the street, throwing Ellery against the Jeep's door.

"I know you like it rough, but I prefer a smoother ride if you know what I mean."

"I really wish I didn't." Gage gritted his teeth and focused on his driving. Even though it was the early hours of the morning, there was still traffic. He didn't need an accident when a life could be at stake. "This is the street. We want forty-eight A. Keep an eye on the mailboxes."

Ellery lowered his window. "I can't see fuck all. Slow down."

Gage slowed to a crawl. "Okay, evens are this side, should be about twenty more properties along."

They reached the right spot. Gage threw the Jeep into park then jumped out. "Uniform should be on the way but we can't wait." He drew his gun.

"I'll just brandish my razor-sharp wit, shall I?" Ellery said, dryly.

"There's a spare vest in the back. Put it on." Gage shrugged into his, slapping the Velcro fastenings closed.

"You do care."

"Landry will be mildly irritated if you get dead. The paperwork will keep me working late for weeks. Let's go. We stick together and you stay behind me. No going all Lone Ranger on me."

"Are you going to kick down the door?"

"The operator has had no luck getting through on the phone. We'll check around the property for any sign of an intruder first."

Gage led the way, Ellery at his shoulder. The house had an open front lawn and a side gate led to a decent-sized yard at the rear. Solar lights studded one side of a patio and their dim glow illuminated the way. Gage checked doors and windows but there was no sign of forced entry. The kitchen was at the rear and he could see that it was tidy, a faint blue luminescence coming from a clock on the microwave.

"Not a lot of action here," Ellery muttered.

"We'll go back around front, try banging on the door."

"Or we could just go in here."

"What the fuck?" Gage gaped as Ellery picked the back door lock then walked into the kitchen without a care in the world. "Jesus." He followed, cursing.

Ellery held a finger to his lips. Gage wanted to shove that finger up a nostril. He elbowed Ellery out of the way then moved through the kitchen to the hall. Everything remained quiet so he made his way up the stairs, giving thanks for the thick runner that cushioned his steps. On the landing, he paused, listening, but there wasn't a sound. He had four doors to choose from, three of which stood ajar. The first led to an empty bedroom, the second to a linen closet. Gage shook his head. If there was anyone in the house, it was a miracle they hadn't been disturbed yet. He hoped the homeowner didn't have a gun. The third door led to what he thought was the master suite, and there was someone sound asleep in the bed, snoring loudly.

Gage debated what to do. If he shook the person awake, he risked scaring them to death and getting the police department sued. If he left without warning the homeowner, he'd be failing in his duty of care. He retreated to find Ellery on the landing. He gestured at the fourth door, indicating that there was no one there. Gage pointed at the stairs and the two of them made their way back down to the hall. They had a look round the ground floor but there was no sign anything was wrong. Gage led the way back outside.

"I have no idea how they slept through that, but it's clear that no one has broken in."

"They could have taken sleeping pills," Ellery said. "Either voluntarily or without knowing it."

"Can you re-lock the door?" Ellery gave Gage a scathing glance. "Fine, I didn't mean to offend your professional sensibilities. Get on with it." The blinking of blue lights in the street told Gage that backup had arrived. He went back to the street to meet them.

"Can you guys hang around here?" He explained that he'd been inside and found nothing out of order, that the homeowner was safe and completely oblivious. "When you see signs of life in the morning, knock on the door and explain what's going on. They shouldn't go to work, okay. We need to track down the next person in the chain." After a few more minutes briefing the cops, Gage returned to his Jeep and Ellery got in next to him.

"We're missing something," Gage muttered, drumming his fingers on the steering wheel.

"I don't remember the last time I slept as deeply as that woman."

"A guilty conscience will do that to you."

"You should do stand-up—you'd bring the house down." Ellery massaged the back of his neck. "Why am I not in bed doing the horizontal tango with Sorrell Sweeting?"

"Because you have a boyfriend who would tie a knot in your dick?"

"Who gave Sorrell the go-ahead to spend the evening with me when they spoke earlier today. Or rather yesterday."

"That open relationship crap you spouted is bullshit. You're as much under Tad's thumb as I am Landry's." Gage glanced at his watch and groaned. "Let's review. The killer has been tracking this piece of furniture from dealer to dealer, killing people on the way, so why not this one? Why is Josephine's owner safely asleep in their bed?"

"Because his objective has changed?" Ellery said. "He knows we're on his trail. Perhaps we're closer than we think."

"So he's more focused on getting to what he's looking for. Does that mean he's going after the next link in the chain? Mr. Lao."

"But Landry wasn't able to get hold of him, and I don't get the impression that Mr. Lao would ignore a phone call from Landry, or that he'd sleep through several calls."

"I'll try again." Gage found the number in his contacts. Mr. Lao answered after two rings.

"Gage, I'm glad you called. Landry left me several garbled messages, but I've been out at a gallery opening and it turned into quite a party. My cell was on silent, and I didn't think to look at it until I got home. I tried to call him back but got no answer. Maggie and I were just having a night cap before heading for bed."

"In that case, Mr. Lao, I want you to get back in your vehicle and drive to a hotel. Don't ask questions and don't stop to collect anything, just go." Gage heard a sharp intake of breath then Mr. Lao telling Maggie to grab her purse. "We're on our way. I'll call you back once we've checked in somewhere and I trust you'll tell me what this is all about then."

Gage heaved a sigh of relief, glad that Mr. Lao trusted him enough to do what he'd been told without question. "That deals with another worry on my list, at least temporarily."

"And it seems that no one was waiting at Mr. Lao's place when he got back, so that leaves us one option."

"And it's the other side of town. Treasure Trove's storage facility behind the Eastern Emporium. If the killer has somehow got ahead of us, that's where he'll be heading."

Ellery frowned. "Oh shit."

"What?"

"How close an eye do you think your friend Carson will be keeping on Landry?" Gage stared at Ellery. "He wouldn't, would he?"

"He fucking would. He won't be able to resist." Gage tossed his cell at Ellery. "Carson is speed dial two." He gunned the engine and shot away down the empty street, did a squealing U-turn then headed back toward Treasure Trove. "What time is it?"

"Almost four. Carson, it's James Ellery. I'm with Gage and I'm putting you on speaker."

"Hey, Carson, sorry to call at this ridiculous hour. Are you guys all okay?"

"Sure, we relocated to your apartment. Petey and I are in the spare room, Sorrell is on the couch. Landry went to bed just before the rest of us."

"Can you go check on him please?"

"Sure." Gage tightened his grip on the wheel while he waited for Carson to report back.

"He's not here, Gage. He must've snuck out."

"Fuck! I should have gotten you to chain him to the damn bed."

"I'm so sorry, Gage. I can't believe I didn't hear him leave."

"Not your fault, Carson. When Landry gets a thought in his head, there's no stopping him. Ellery and I are on our way to the Eastern Emporium. We are twenty minutes out."

"I can be over there in five."

"No, you should stay with Petey and Sorrell."

"Fuck that. Don't be stupid, Gage. I can lock them inside. They'll be safe in the apartment. I'm already on my way—don't try to talk me out of it."

"My spare piece is in the gun safe under our bed." Gage gave Carson the combination. "There's ammunition in there too. I need to call it in and get backup on the way. I'll get back to you as quickly as I can, don't do anything to put yourself at risk. We think the killer could be on the way to the storage place too."

"You can catch me up when you get here."

"Be careful, Carson. This killer is ruthless." Gage nodded at Ellery to disconnect. "Try Landry for me."

"It's going to voicemail."

"Of course it is. I swear that disobedient little brat will be the death of me."

Ellery snorted. "Landry has nine lives. He'll be fine."

Gage wasn't so sure. Landry's luck had been tested too many times already.

The drive seemed interminable, and Gage's nerves were taut as bowstrings by the time he pulled up outside Treasure Trove. He left the Jeep there then he and Ellery crossed the street to the Eastern Emporium.

"I don't know where I'm going," Gage admitted. "It's around back somewhere but I've never been there." He led the way through the small parking lot behind the store.

"That has to be it," Ellery whispered. "It's the only building big enough to be a store. There has to be another way in."

"We may need your lock picking skills again," Gage said. "And there's something I never thought I'd need to say. I wonder where Carson is."

Sirens wailed from the street and the sound of speeding vehicles echoed through the early morning quiet. Lights came on above the store. "Well fuck. There goes any chance of a surprise entry." Gage paused. "Can you go head off Mr. Agarwal? He's the Emporium's owner, and I'm certain he'll be out here in a few minutes. Then talk to the cops when they arrive and keep them away until I give the all clear. I don't want this turning into a hostage situation."

"If there's anyone in there. It's very quiet."

Gage had been thinking the same. He hadn't spotted any unfamiliar vehicles on the street and there was no sound coming from the building. He parted company with Ellery then made his way around the structure, triggering security lights as he went. There was little point in trying to remain stealthy. He found the access door right away. It was wide open, jammed into a clump of grass and nettles. Gage's instinct told him something was up, so he took extra care as he moved forward, listening hard before flicking the light switch. The cavernous space filled with a yellowish glow cast by a half-dozen strip lights suspended from the roof.

"Carson. Damn it." Gage spotted his friend's boots first, then his legs, then the rest of him. He was on the floor near the far wall. Gage ran over to him. He knelt on the dusty floor and felt for a pulse. At his touch, Carson groaned before lifting a hand to his temple. His fingers came away bloody.

"Gage? What the hell happened?"

"I was about to ask you the same thing. Can you sit up?"

"Sure. Hell. My fucking head hurts."

"You're bleeding, idiot, stop prodding it. Did you see Landry?"

"Yes. I came over here and the door at the back was open. It was dark, but I could see movement. Landry was on the floor, half in that chest over there. I didn't see the other guy until he jumped me. He must have heard me coming. Landry yelled, tried to warn me, but he came at me so fast. I was distracted, trying to see if Landry was okay, and the fucker clocked me with something. I remember hitting the floor, then nothing. Where are they?"

"You're the only person in here. They've gone. Whoever it was has taken Landry."

Carson attempted to get up. Gage helped him to his feet. "I should never have let you come over here."

"I've managed to make a complete mess of the whole evening. I can't even babysit a few subs."

"Carson, it's not your fault. A bunch of puppies would be easier to wrangle. I'm just glad you're okay, but we need to get you seen by a medic."

"I'm good. I can't have been out for long. You must have missed them by minutes."

"Story of my fucking life." Gage glanced around. It was easy to see where the Emporium's stock ended and Treasure Trove's began, because the furniture was all covered with dustsheets. One area had been disturbed. A few pieces of furniture had been uncovered, the covers strewn around. There was a huge wooden trunk with iron banding, a table, a leather armchair. Gage made his way over to the piece that looked most like a bureau-style desk. Several of its drawers had been removed and the cupboards were hanging open. On closer inspection he could see that two secret compartments had been exposed but they were both empty.

"Fuck, Landry. Where are you?" Gage wanted to punch someone in the worst way. Unfortunately, James Ellery wasn't in range.

Gage escorted Carson outside. "I need to let everyone know what's going on." Prisha's father, Prisha and a bunch of cops were milling around on the other side of the parking lot. Gage strode across to them, Carson on his heels.

"What's going on, Detective Roskam?" One of the cops approached him.

Gage brought him up to date with a quick summary of events. "There's no one inside now, but we'll need to get the place dusted for prints. I'd also like the proprietor to look to see if he can spot anything missing, though the Emporium stock seems to be untouched. It's…"

"Gage!"

"Mr. Lao?" Landry's boss ran over to him. "What are you doing here? You're supposed to be safely tucked away in a hotel." Gage huffed his frustration. "Why is it that no one ever does what I tell them to? Don't answer that." He aimed that at Ellery, who grinned.

"I've been trying to get hold of Landry and he's not answering his phone," Mr. Lao said. "Then I called Petey, and he gave me some long, garbled story about killers and antiques and clues, and that Carson had gone somewhere with a gun… I had no idea what he was going on about, so I decided to come over. You should know that he and some other young man are standing on the sidewalk outside Treasure Trove and there's quite a crowd gathering. Carson, my boy, you don't look well."

"Fuck my life." Gage went over to the cops. "Can you go do crowd control on the street? Direct the crime scene guys when they get here and does anyone have latex gloves I can borrow, because I'm going to take a look inside and I don't want to walk all the way back to my Jeep."

"Make that two pairs," Ellery threw in.

"I'll go with the cops," Carson said. "I'll make sure Petey and Sorrell go back inside. I'll get them making drinks, keep them busy. I'm sure everyone could use a coffee."

"Make sure somebody looks at that head," Gage grumbled. "What a fucking mess. I need a holiday. Gonna take Landry some place remote where even he can't get into trouble, sleep for a week then strap him to a flat surface and fuck him till he screams."

"Sounds good. Need a third?" Ellery asked.

"You were not supposed to be listening to that."

"What about me?"

"No, Mr. Lao. Nor you. Oh my God."

"Entertaining, Detective, but maybe oversharing a little." One of the cops thrust latex gloves at Gage.

"Did the entire world listen in to my private conversation?" Gage grabbed the gloves.

Ellery took a pair too. "You were conversing with yourself, Gage. Out loud. What did you expect?"

"A modicum of privacy?"

"Then maybe internalize the angsty monologues, okay?"

"Some psycho has my boyfriend and we are no closer to solving this fucking case. I'm entitled to a rant."

"Think positive. From what Carson said, the killer could have dealt with Landry right here. He didn't. Landry is probably convincing him that he should become a monk or something, at a really remote monastery, with a vow of silence." Ellery snapped his second glove into place. "So how about we take a look inside…unless you have something better to do?"

Gage took a breath. His fear for Landry was clouding his judgment. "I fucking hate it when you're right. Mr. Lao, if you could come inside with us. Don't touch anything. I need you to tell me if you spot something out of place or missing. Prisha, you and your dad should go inside. This is going to take a while."

"What about Landry? Where is he?" Prisha had her hands on her hips and was looking stubborn.

"We don't know where he is right now." Gage tried to pacify her. "Try not to worry too much. You know Landry."

"I do and that's the problem." Prisha tugged her dad's arm. "Come on, Poppa, we'll head over to Treasure Trove, make sure Carson is okay."

"Okay, let's go."

Gage, Mr. Lao and Ellery went back inside the store, walking over to the area that had been disturbed. Mr. Lao wandered around muttering about the mess.

"There's nothing missing, Gage. It would be tough to get anything out of here without opening the roller shutters and most of these pieces take two men to lift. I'm assuming the secretaire is the item causing all this grief?"

Gage nodded. "We weren't sure. It was a lead we were following but everything points to something of value having been hidden inside it."

"Well, in that case you should know that only two of the three secret compartments are open."

Gage stared at him but Ellery was already examining the piece. "How intriguing. I can see where the releases were for these other sections."

"Press the carved rose on the corner of the letter rack," Mr. Lao instructed.

Ellery pushed the intricately crafted flower and a panel in the back of the bureau dropped forward, revealing a space behind it. "There's nothing here," Ellery said. "Wait a minute...there's a scrap of paper. It's a corner of a luggage label, I think. It has PA written on it." Ellery chuckled. "In purple glitter pen. I don't think that's contemporary to the desk somehow."

"Landry." Gage frowned. "I'll get this place searched properly. Meanwhile, you and I need to think about what Landry's clue means."

When Gage, Ellery and Mr. Lao reached the street, they found Treasure Trove open for business. Cops milled outside, holding mugs of coffee, others were crowding into the cafe next door. Inside the store, Petey had Mr. Lao's kettle and tea-making kit spread on the cash desk. Sorrel was handing out bacon sandwiches wrapped in foil, which must have come from the cafe. Someone had pulled together a collection of chairs in front of the cash desk and that was where Gage slumped with a sigh. Mr. Lao went to sort himself out what he called a decent cup of proper tea. Ellery grabbed a sandwich, which he ate as if he hadn't had a meal in days. Gage took the mug of coffee Ellery handed him.

"Christ, I'm tired. I don't recommend this staying up all night gig."

Ellery came over to join him. "Where's Carson? How's he doing?"

"He has a big lump on his head, but he's mainly annoyed that someone got the jump on him. I'm happy he didn't have to use the gun though. He's used to saving people and he thinks he's let Landry down. He went up to the apartment to get sugar. He should be back any minute." Gage scowled into his coffee. "He went into an unpredictable situation and from what he told me, he couldn't have done anything more without risking Landry's life. He did a brave thing and I'm grateful he was here. If he hadn't disturbed the killer, who knows what might have happened."

Carson made his way over and handed the sugar he was carrying to Sorrel. "Nice of you to say, but I'm still playing over in my head what I could have done to get Landry out of there." He took the seat next to Gage while Ellery leaned against the cash desk.

"Are we anywhere close to identifying who this guy is?" Petey asked.

"He was wearing a balaclava," Carson said. "I didn't get a look at him."

"Landry did leave us a clue," Gage said, producing the scrap of luggage label Ellery had found in the secretaire. "Anyone have any idea what the letters 'p' and 'a' might stand for?"

Ellery, who had finished the last of his sandwich, licked his fingers. "From what I remember they don't match the initials of anyone we've been interested in."

"Did you say 'p' and 'a', Gage?" Sorrel put down the plate he was carrying.

"That's right."

"Then what if it stands for Penton's Antiquarium?"

"Could be." Gage's head hurt. He mulled over why Landry might have tried to direct him to the store but his brain was sluggish. "Sorrel, when we were leaving Scorch, you called your colleagues to warn them about what was happening, didn't you? Who did you ring?"

"Chet and Marla from the store. Marla said she was going to take the kids and go stay with her sister for a few days. Chet just said thanks for the heads-up and that he'd be careful. You don't think…?"

Gage's mind cleared. "You also told me that both Marla and Chet left the Antiquarium after I interviewed you all. How long had Chet been working for Penton?"

"A few months," Sorrel said. "The previous senior sales guy retired, so we had an opening. Penton said he was introduced to Chet at an estate sale and offered him the job. He said he had a ruthless streak when he was bidding and he was definitely an excellent salesperson, especially with the ladies. I was never sure how long he'd stick around though once he realized what Penton was like."

Gage and Ellery exchanged glances. "Chet. No wonder he's been ahead of us every step of the way. He would have had time to get to the Antiquarium's storage facility before me that day. When he realized the desk wasn't there, he would have had access to Penton's records to find out who it had been sold to."

Sorrel was white. He sat down heavily. "You mean I've been working with a killer?"

"It seems likely," Gage said. "Landry wouldn't have known his name, but he may have given something away that let Landry work out that he was on the staff at Penton's. He couldn't have had much time to write a message so all he could manage was the initials of the store. I'll get someone to start digging into Chet's background."

"How about his car?" Ellery said. "What did he drive, Sorrel?"

"A Lexus. But surely he wouldn't be so dumb as to use his own vehicle?"

"I doubt he would have had time after your phone call to make alternative arrangements. He would have thought that this was the end of the trail. What he didn't account for was Landry." Gage glanced around his friends taking in their drawn expressions and slumped shoulders. "Landry has given us what we need. Now we do our job and find him."

Chapter Seventeen

Landry's terror built by the second. He'd been in some tight spots before, but he'd never been so certain that if he didn't take action, he would die, and not in a quick, walk-into-the-light kind of way. Balaclava man wanted information that only Landry had. Landry kept picturing Arthur Penton's corpse, his bloody clothing and Gage telling him that the poor man had been stabbed several times. Landry didn't want any more holes in his body, he was quite happy with the ones he had. He squeezed his eyes shut, trying to close off visions of what his abductor might do with a knife.

Pull yourself together, Landry Carran. You're too young and far too pretty to die. Not that old, ugly people deserve it more… Gah, calm down and think!

The car was slowing, Landry was sure of it, and he could hear the sounds of heavy traffic and the horns of frustrated, impatient drivers. *It's now or never.* Fear made him clumsy but he managed to release the safety catch on the trunk. He'd expected it to bang up, giving him moments to escape, but it didn't. Instead, a crack of light showed it was open. Landry stretched his cramped limbs as best he could. He peeked through the gap, sucking in cold air, trying to work out where he was. The vehicle behind was a Metro bus. Office buildings loomed to either side. He had to be downtown somewhere, heading in the direction of the river he thought. A car horn sounded close by, making him jump. He grinned — for once, the delights of Seattle traffic would work for him. The car slowed even more, and he caught the sound of a jackhammer in the distance. A cement truck pulled past the bus, its load churning.

Construction. Landry realized they must be approaching the spot where a new hotel was being built. The site had made the local news because the traffic calming measures around it had been causing major bottlenecks. Seattle's mayor had weighed in, probably because his office wasn't far away.

The car was crawling. Landry opened the trunk a few inches, then performed a graceless flop onto the road. His hip hit the ground first. He rolled once, scrambled to his feet and dodged to one side. The bus applied its air brakes with a hiss and as he dodged through the next lane of traffic to the median Landry caught a glimpse of the driver's startled face. Landry didn't wait. He scrambled up the low, grassy bank then ran full pelt down the nearest street without looking back.

He took the first corner he came to, wanting to be out of sight of the road. He risked a quick glance over his shoulder, lost his balance and fell. "Ow! Fuck!"

"Wow that was quite a tumble. Are you hurt, young man?"

From his hands and knees, Landry looked up into a kindly, wrinkled face framed by an impressive mane of gray hair. "I need to get to a phone. Do you have one?"

"Name is Bill. Don't hold with them new-fangled devices but the boys at the Coffee Bean are glued to the damn things. It's just up a ways." Bill hauled Landry to his feet. "You look like you've been in the wars, son."

Landry trailed after Bill, limping. "I'm Landry. I was kidnapped by a killer searching for evidence proving the death of some rich dude in England wasn't from natural causes. I just escaped from the trunk of his car."

Bill turned to stare at him. "You don't look high. Why do I get the feeling you ain't yanking my chain?"

Landry shrugged. "Why else would I be up at this hour?"

"I can think of a thousand more likely reasons. Walk of shame for one."

"In this outfit?" Landry gestured at his now torn and filthy clothing. "I made it out of the car less than five minutes ago. He could be following me."

"Traffic is pretty snarled up."

"That's why I'm still in one piece. Mostly." Standing still meant Landry started noticing various aches and pains. He grimaced.

"Let's get you into the Bean, then I'll take a walk down the street."

"I don't want to drag you into this, Bill."

"Son, this is the most interesting start to a day I've had in years."

The Coffee Bean proved to be a tiny, hole-in-the-wall coffee shop with three tables and a counter adorned with rainbow bunting.

"Morning, Bill, who's your buddy?" The bearded guy behind the counter was huge and broad. Muscles bulged from a T-shirt Landry guessed was holding it together through willpower alone. There was a picture of a Care Bear on the front dressed in a leather harness and the slogan 'Daddy Bear'.

"Boy here is Landry. He needs to make a call, Tank. Bit of a crisis going on."

Landry dropped into a free seat and let Bill give a quick explanation to the assorted customers and the café's proprietor whose bushy eyebrows were gradually disappearing into his hairline.

"You're not shitting me?"

"I believe him," Bill said, "and if I'm not very much mistaken, he's family."

"Love your T-shirt," Landry said, confirming Bill's suspicions.

"Well boy, you done look like a semi rolled over you. You need a bandage?"

Landry looked from Tank to Bill, took in their concerned expressions and burst into tears. "I want Gage," he wailed.

"Can you take care of him, Tank?" Bill handed Landry a pristine spotted handkerchief. "I'm gonna take a walk down the street and check that no one is heading this way who looks out of place."

"Breath of fresh air would suit me too, Bill." One of the Coffee Bean's other customers pushed his chair back. When he stood, he was as tall as Tank and wearing heavy work boots, battered jeans and a Hi-Viz vest over a plaid shirt.

"I'd appreciate that, Francis."

"No problem." Francis had a quick word with the other men at his table, who shuffled their chairs until they formed a barrier between Landry and the door.

"Ain't no one getting in here who shouldn't," Francis said before striding out with Bill.

Landry wiped his nose with the back of his sleeve. "Sorry, I'm gross. I've been up all night and I kinda did something dumb. If the bad guy doesn't get me, my Dom…I mean my boyfriend will probably kill me anyway."

Tank came around the counter and held out his cell. "Call your Dom, Landry. He must be frantic."

Landry punched in the number. "Gage, it's me…" He couldn't stop the tears.

"Landry, thank God. Where are you? Are you safe?"

"I'm in a Coffee Bean… I mean I'm in a shop, place with coffee… There are people…"

"You're not making any sense."

Tank took the cell out of Landry's shaking hand. "Hey, the name's Tank Jones over at the Coffee Bean coffee shop on Archer. Landry's here, he safe but he's a bit beat up and I think he's in shock. He says he escaped from a car and that someone might be after him."

"I'm Detective Gage Roskam, Landry is my partner, and he was taken by someone I would dearly like to talk to."

"Do you want to come fetch him, or would you prefer us to bring him to you?"

"Are you sure he's safe with you? The guy that's after him is ruthless."

"Ain't nobody getting near him, Detective. We look after our own here, if you know what I mean. You have a sweet sub. You're a lucky man."

"He's a bundle of trouble, Tank, but worth it. Keep him safe for me."

"Don't you worry none. Several people here heard his story. They ain't letting anyone near him, believe me."

Tank handed the cell back to Landry. "Sir? I think I found a whole pack of bears. Actually a sleuth would be the correct collective term."

"Well, that's good, sweetheart, and I learned something new. I want you to stay right there. I'm coming to get you."

"Are you mad at me?"

"I'm not mad. We need to discuss your understanding of obedience, but I'm not mad. I can't tell you how relieved I am that you're safe."

"I think the killer is someone who works at the Antiquarium. He said that somebody had called to let him know where the secretaire was and all I could think about was Sorrell calling his colleagues when we were at Scorch."

"We found your clue, love. Sorrell suggested the Antiquarium and Ellery worked it out. The guy's name is Chet, though I doubt it's his real name. We've got people on the case tracking his car and several possible locations he might head for."

"I found a bottle hidden in a secret compartment in the desk. I was right."

"Yes, you were, but please remember which one of us is in law enforcement and which one is in antiques."

"Yes, Sir."

"This bottle, do you have it with you?"

"No. I heard someone coming after I found it. I hid it. I thought I'd be able to buy some time because the killer would want the bottle but then Carson came in. Is he okay? Chet caught him by surprise, hit him with something. He went down hard."

"He's fine. Annoyed with himself and he has a lump on his head, but Petey is administering first aid."

"You might want to stop that, Sir. Petey tried to take a splinter out of my finger once and nearly cut it off."

"I sometimes wonder how the pair of you are still alive. I can't believe I'm telling you this but eat something sweet. The sugar will help because you're likely in shock. Where did you hide the bottle?"

Landry giggled. "In a toilet."

"Excuse me?"

"A toilet. Well, a commode. An American Classical period commode in mahogany to be precise. With a marble-inset top, scrolled backsplash and sides. I know, 'cause it's one of the few things Mr. Lao let me buy. I found it at an antique fair, and it sold super quick. We're holding it for a client."

"You hid a valuable piece of evidence in a toilet?"

"I did. Cool, huh? I'm a genius. I had to find somewhere real fast. It was right next to the desk. Ellery will know what it is when he sees it." Landry visualized Gage rolling his eyes.

"Okay, we'll go retrieve it. I'm gonna go now but I won't be long. And, Landry?"

"Yes, Sir?"

"If you leave that coffee shop, you'll be an old man before you get to know what an orgasm feels like again. Understand?"

"Eat sugar, Sir. Yes, Sir." Landry handed the cell back to Tank. "He's on his way. He said I had to eat something sugary, and he never says that so he must be worried."

"That's good—that he's on his way, not that he's worried I mean. How about you wash up in the restroom. I'll fetch the first aid supplies so I can patch you up then you can have your pick of the pastries and a big mug of coffee."

In a spontaneous rush of gratitude, Landry gave Tank a hug. "You're so sweet!"

"Aw shucks."

Twenty minutes later, Landry found himself sitting at one of the Coffee Bean's tables, working on one of the best chocolate brownies he'd ever tasted. His various cuts and scrapes had been bandaged and Tank had proved to be an excellent barista. At least as good as Mary. An audience of Tank's customers had built as they'd come in for their breakfast or morning brew, and they all wanted to hear Landry's story. The murmurings of concern and protective growls from the bunch of men who were uniformly huge and hairy was comforting. Landry had never seen so many impressive beards in one place before or quite such a colorful collection of plaid shirts.

"Do you guys all work construction?" he asked. He soon learned that his new friends included a surveyor, a preschool teacher, a florist and a pharmacist. Their sartorial choices reflected their warm, caring personalities. "I will never make assumptions based on red and black checks again."

Bill and his companion returned from their survey of the street with nothing to report. Landry allowed himself to relax and one by one, his new friends drifted off to their jobs all with standing invitations to visit Treasure Trove any time they wanted. Tank, who had been working behind the counter, joined Landry and Bill at the table. "That's the early rush over. Just time to take a breather for a few minutes before the commuter crowd start arriving. I guess your detective will be here any minute, Landry."

"I hope so." Landry picked at the edge of the bandage covering his grazed palm.

"Stop messing with that," Tank warned. "You need to keep it covered so it doesn't get infected. I didn't pick those bits of gravel out of it for you to ruin my good work."

"You and Gage are gonna be friends," Landry said. "I know it." He thought to himself that he would like to bring Sorrell along to meet Tank. The man had a good heart and needed someone of his own to look after. Sorrell definitely needed a keeper and someone to be attached to that wasn't James Ellery.

"Speak of the devil." It was Ellery who pushed through the door of the Coffee Bean, Gage close behind him. Landry got up so fast he tilted his chair and Tank had to catch it.

"Sir!" Landry threw himself into Gage's arms with a sob. For a moment, Gage held him tight without speaking then pushed him away a few inches.

"Let me look at you."

"I'm sorry about your sweater," Landry said, sticking his finger through one of several holes in the garment.

"We'll get to the topic of why you're wearing my clothes instead of your own later," Gage said. "I'm just relieved the holes aren't in you."

"These are my new friends, Tank and Bill." Landry introduced the men who both shook Gage's hand. "This is my boyfriend, Detective Gage Roskam, and his partner, James Ellery."

"It's a pleasure, gentlemen," Ellery said.

"You don't sound like you're from around here," Bill commented. "I spent some time stationed in England. You know the airbase near Croughton?"

"As it happens, I am familiar with that area," Ellery said. "We must get together another time and discuss all things English. My partner here doesn't even appreciate a decent cup of tea and is very confused about what a biscuit is supposed to look like."

Bill chortled. "Don't encourage him," Gage said. "He's insufferable enough as it is."

"Did you find the bottle, Sir?" Landry asked.

"We did. You were right about Ellery knowing an old toilet when he saw one."

"Commode!" Landry and Ellery shouted at the same time.

"You say tom-ay-toe…"

"When the correct pronunciation is toh-mah-toe," Ellery interrupted, and Gage responded with a pained sigh.

"Tank, can I get two coffees to go, please? Three shots, maybe four. It's been one long-assed night."

"Sure." Tank fired up the coffee machine. "I was wondering why you were wearing leather pants…is that usual plain clothes for Seattle detectives?"

Landry giggled at the twinkle in Tank's eye. "Before all this went down, Tank, we were at Scorch enjoying a night out. You should wear leather more often though, Sir. It's hot."

"You should," Ellery added with a shrug.

"I can just hear the comments in the squad room," Gage muttered. "That'll be a hell no." He took the take-out cup Tank offered him. "You see what I have to put up with?" He handed the other cup to Ellery.

"Hey, I agree with them."

"Time to get you home, Landry." Gage swigged his coffee. "I'm too tired to debate the merits of my leather pants."

"Don't I get more coffee, Sir?" Landry bounced.

There was a chorus of "no" from everyone present. Gage hustled Landry toward the door. "I appreciate you guys taking care of him," Gage said. He handed Tank a card with his contact details. "In case you need it. We'll be back for statements at some point when I'm not in danger of falling asleep on my feet."

"Come back for a meal," Tank said. "You're all welcome any time."

Bill followed them out. "It was nice to meet you, young Landry. I'll be dropping by the store some time, you can be sure of that."

Landry gave Bill a hug. "Thanks for saving me, Bill. I got new friends out of all this. So worth it."

"I think you could be a dangerous friend to have. I like that." His eyes gleamed. "Take care of yourself."

Giddy with fatigue and edging toward hysteria, Landry clambered into Gage's Jeep. He curled up on the back seat and drifted off before they'd even pulled away.

* * * *

Gage carried Landry up the stairs to their apartment. Ellery held the door so that he could get Landry into the bedroom without disturbing him. Gently, Gage took off Landry's shoes and socks before tucking him into bed. He didn't bother with the rest of his clothes, dirty though they were, because he didn't want to wake him. Asleep, the worry lines were smoothed from his face.

"Christ, he looks so young."

"You sit with him awhile. I'll go make coffee."

Gage acknowledged Ellery with a nod. He couldn't take his eyes off Landry's sleeping form. He never wanted to let him out of his sight again, though he knew he was being irrational. He rubbed at his eyes, exhausted beyond measure. The temptation to crawl into bed beside Landry rode Gage hard, but he had work to do. He brushed a strand of blond hair away from Landry's eyes. "I've not been doing a very good job of keeping you safe, have I? That's going to change." He crept from the room, leaving the door open. If Landry woke, he'd likely be disoriented and Gage wanted to hear if he cried out.

He found Ellery leaning on the kitchen counter, staring at the coffeepot as if he didn't quite know what to do with it. A floorboard creaked under Gage's weight and Ellery started.

"I always wondered if it was possible to sleep standing up with your eyes open. Now I know." He scooped coffee grounds into the filter then added boiling water. The aroma of fresh coffee immediately wafted through the room.

"I don't think there's enough caffeine on the planet to keep me awake for much longer," Gage admitted. "We should plan our next move then get some shut eye. You can use the spare bedroom."

Ellery grabbed two mugs that had been sitting on the draining board. He filled them and handed one to Gage.

"Let's take these into the living room." Gage led the way to the couch where he and Ellery sat side-by-side, sipping their drinks in silence for a good five minutes. "This isn't finished, is it?" Gage placed his mug on a side table with deliberate care.

"Not while Chet is out there. He has unfinished business."

"The first job is to identify him. I'll get some people onto obtaining samples for DNA analysis. We don't have his car, but we know where he was working and Mrs. Penton senior should be able to provide a home address. I'd guess everything we know about him is fake, but DNA won't lie. We should also be able to lift prints from something and get a photograph from his employment record. If he's on a criminal database anywhere, we'll find him."

"I've been thinking about the bottle." Ellery drummed his fingers on his knee. "I want to run an idea past you."

"Go ahead but bear in mind I'm so tired that when I wake up I'll think it was a dream and you'll have to tell me all over again. In fact, hold that thought. I need to find Mr. Lao and talk to Petey and Carson. It's past time to open the store. I thought I might attempt to convince them to close for the day."

"Good luck with that. You want me to come with you?"

"No. Get some sleep. I'll do the same when I get back and set my alarm. "

"I'll forgive you if you have to dump a bucket of cold water over me to wake me."

"Oh don't tempt me."

Gage left the apartment and stomped up a set of stairs. He knocked on Petey's apartment door and wasn't surprised when Carson opened it.

"You're back. How's Landry?"

"Sleeping. A bit battered. Would you believe he jumped out of the trunk of a moving car? Slow moving, thank Christ. Then, Landry being Landry found himself a rainbow-colored café full of bears who were protecting him like a new-born cub when I arrived."

Carson chortled. "Petey will be relieved. I managed to get him to sleep but only after convincing him to have a tot of brandy in his hot chocolate. That boy cannot take his drink. He was out like a light."

"How about Mr. Lao, he didn't go home, did he? The killer is still out there."

"No. After you and James left, he went to his hotel. He'll probably be here shortly because he said he'd be back to open up. He said to let the boys sleep in."

"And Sorrell?"

"Snoring on our couch. I didn't think it was a good idea to send him home."

"Thanks, Carson. I was in such a hurry to get to Landry that I didn't think to leave instructions for anyone else. I'm glad you're here."

"No problem."

"What about you, have you had any sleep? How's your head?"

"I dozed but I didn't think it wise that everyone should be sound asleep. I'm used to keeping strange hours on my shifts and my head is fine, though I'm glad it's under a helmet at work."

Gage snorted. "When are you on shift again?"

"This evening. My watch is on nights for the next month."

"Oh, that'll please Petey."

"Don't I know it? He's getting used to it but I'm considering making some changes."

"It's a balancing act, isn't it, caring for someone?"

"They're worth it though. No question. I always thought submission was the ultimate gift but until

Petey let me into his life, I didn't truly understand. Listen to me, what a sap."

"You're not the only one that's fallen under that spell," Gage admitted. "I couldn't imagine ever finding the right man to collar, but I can't wait to get that strip of leather around Landry's neck permanently."

"Pretty sure it's some kind of witchcraft but I don't really care," Carson said, grinning.

"Same." Gage swayed. "Shit, I'm getting too old to deal with all-nighters. Ellery is at our place, and we're going to grab a couple hours' sleep before we get going again. Do you mind letting Mr. Lao know when he arrives? We should let Landry and Petey sleep as long as possible."

"Sure. I can hang with Mr. Lao in the store for a while then sleep this afternoon. Go lie down before you collapse."

Gage nodded. He trudged back down the stairs. In the apartment, he found that Ellery had cleared up their coffee things and when Gage snuck a look in the spare room, he found him sound asleep on the bed, still fully dressed. Gage padded into his bedroom where Landry was sprawled, taking up most of the bed. Gage stripped to his underwear then crawled beneath the covers, nudging Landry's limbs to one side. He lay on his back, staring at the ceiling, waiting for sleep to claim him. Landry snuffled and Gage thought he heard his name then Landry rolled so that he was lying half on Gage half on the bed. He was still wearing jeans and Gage's sweater, so the heat soaked into Gage's skin. He held Landry tight, closed his eyes and blanked his mind. Some sleep might just inspire him to come up with a decent plan.

Chapter Eighteen

Landry came to in a slow drift of awareness. His awakening didn't improve as his body informed him that it didn't appreciate the previous day's abuse. He stuck out a hand to pat the bed where Gage was supposed to be. The sheets were still warm.

"Gage?" His voice croaked. "I sound like a thirsty frog. Need coffee."

"And since when is that different from any other day?" Gage, stark naked, wandered into the bedroom. "There's a pot brewing in the kitchen."

"Am I still asleep? I'm having a spectacular dream and there's a gorgeous naked cop in my bedroom. I think he's about to ravish me."

"You're awake, sweetheart. Suffering from a lack of caffeine but not hallucinations. Sadly, we don't have time for the ravishing part."

"What time is it?" Landry sat bolt upright. "Why am I dressed?"

"When I brought you back here earlier, you were already sound asleep. I didn't want to wake you by taking your clothes off. It's early afternoon. Considering everything you went through overnight, oversleeping is understandable."

"Oh my God, the store! I need to go open up."

"Stop panicking. Mr. Lao is in control with Carson as a very capable assistant. Petey is sleeping in too and Sorrell's with him."

"What about Ellery?"

"In the kitchen making you something to eat."

Landry slumped back on his pillows. "I could get used to this. Two Doms waiting on me hand and foot."

Gage scowled and put his hands on his hips. "Let's get one thing straight, Ellery is not a permanent fixture in this apartment and never will be."

"You're never hotter than when you're all stern and possessive, Sir. Fuck me? Please."

Landry scrambled out of his clothes and the instant he was naked Gage crawled over him, already reaching for the lube on the bedside cabinet. He hoisted Landry's legs onto his shoulders. "No time for romance."

"Want you in me, not hearts and flowers."

Gage slathered his cock with lube then prepped Landry's hole with a few deft strokes of his finger. "You have a graze on your ass," Gage muttered as he pushed into Landry's willing body.

"I'd ask you to kiss it better, but I'm not sure that's physically possible at the moment." Landry closed his eyes, relishing the sensation of Gage's rock-hard cock filling him completely. He was a bit lightheaded already and that increased when Gage began to move. "Harder, Sir."

Grunting, Gage didn't hold back. He gave Landry exactly what he wanted, what he needed and when he came, filling Landry's channel with heat, Landry came too, not even needing a touch from Gage's hand to pull him over the edge. Instead, Landry reached for Gage, digging his fingers into Gage's hips, dragging him deeper. His need for connection was overpowering even as Gage softened inside him.

"You're gonna have to let me go at some point, love." Gage sounded amused.

"Don't wanna."

"Not even for coffee?"

"Well, okay then." Landry capitulated, shifting his legs from Gage's shoulders, letting him sit back on his haunches. "I needed that so bad."

"Me too." Gage cleaned himself up with a handful of tissues. He went to dab at the splatters of cum on Landry's belly.

"Don't bother. I'm gonna jump in the shower real quick." Landry didn't really want to move, but he wanted to catch up with his friends and find out what was going on. He could also smell bacon.

Gage pulled on thigh hugging jeans and a soft pullover. "I'll leave you to it."

"How long have you been up?"

"Ellery and I grabbed a couple hours' sleep after we got back, but we've been working since. I needed a shower though, so we took a break. If you hadn't surfaced of your own accord, I would have woken you."

"That's good. If I slept much longer, I'd be hopeless tonight."

"I'll bring you up to speed as much as I'm able over brunch. Or is it lunch?"

"Early afternoon, it must be linner, somewhere between lunch and dinner. I think I just invented a new thing. Go me."

Gage shook his head. "And on that note, I'm going back to work."

"Someone has no respect for my natural inventiveness," Landry grumbled, hauling himself off the bed. Various parts of his body ached but other than a few scrapes and bruises, he'd gotten out of his recent adventures with relatively little damage. He still spent ages in the shower, scrubbing every bit of his body, wanting to get rid of any lingering traces of car trunk odor. He cleaned his teeth twice then gargled with mouthwash, remembering the disgusting gag that had been shoved in his mouth. He took the time to blow dry his hair, because for some reason he was a little cold. He put on his thickest pair of jeans, T-shirt and a roll neck sweater. Thick socks and old tennis shoes completed the ensemble. His reflection revealed dark rings beneath his eyes, pale skin and the tracing of a bruise down one side of his face. His lip was also a bit swollen. "I'll either scare the customers away, or attract sympathy purchases," he mumbled before wandering through to the living room.

Gage and Ellery were already seated. There was a place set for him, a mug of steaming coffee already poured, a chunky bacon sandwich sitting on a plate next to it. Landry slid onto his seat and, without saying anything, devoured the food and slurped down the coffee. He poured another mug from the pot then sat back with a sigh.

"It's official. I can confirm that I am indeed alive." Gage and Ellery were both staring at him. "What are you two looking at?"

"I'm not sure," Ellery said. "I don't think I've ever seen a bacon sandwich disappear quite that fast. I'm impressed."

"I worked up an appetite." Landry blinked at Gage then licked his lips.

Gage cleared his throat and made a grab for the coffee pot. Ellery grinned. "Ah, I see, you've been leading Gage astray. I've been trying to do the same but for some reason he doesn't rise to my bait."

"The only bait he's rising to is mine," Landry snapped. "Got it?"

Ellery inclined his head very slightly. "Can't blame me for trying."

"The only thing you're trying is my patience," Gage said.

Giggling, Landry swallowed more coffee. "Catch me up with everything. What did I miss?"

Gage rolled his shoulders, making the joints audibly crunch. Landry winced.

"The man who attacked you, and we assume the killer, is Chet Oram, a sales guy from Penton's Antiquarium. We don't know if that's his real name and I have people at the precinct looking into him."

"Oh my God, is Sorrel okay?" Landry asked.

"Firmly installed in Carson and Petey's apartment. He slept on the couch."

"That's good. What does this Oram look like? He was wearing a ski mask or balaclava when he nabbed me in the storeroom. Not a good look. And when I jumped out of the car, I only got a very brief glance at the back of his head."

Ellery brought up a picture on his cell and showed it to Landry. Landry went cold. "I know him! I mean not know him know him. I've met him. He was in the store."

"When?" Gage didn't look happy.

"I mentioned him to you before. It was the day Carson finished his rotation. Carson came to the store around lunchtime and I gave Petey the afternoon off. I'd been doing a bit of research on the computer — Landry eyed Gage — "and spooked myself a bit. I went to close up about five minutes early and somebody shoved open the door. The handle banged my arm." He rubbed at where the bruise had been. "The guy seemed harmless. I let him in. He had a quick look around then said he'd come back with his wife. With hindsight, it was a bit odd."

"And you're sure it was the same man?" Gage asked.

"Absolutely, though his hair was a different color and he was wearing a hat. He also had a straggly mustache. I have a good memory for faces. It helps to remember the customers when they come in, they like that."

"He must have been searching for the desk," Ellery said.

"It's a wonder he didn't try anything else." Gage frowned. "Did he ask you any questions?"

"No and come to think of it, a PD cruiser passed by outside, gave a quick blast of its siren and flashing lights. He left straight away and I locked up after him. When I looked out of the window there was no sign of him on the street and the cops had gone."

"I'll check it out with the patrol guys. There's a slight chance they may have seen somebody leaving the store."

"It sounds like you had a narrow escape there, Landry." Ellery didn't sound happy about that.

Landry downed his mug of coffee in swift gulps, not wanting to think about what might have happened if he'd spent more time alone in the store with the man he now knew to be Chet Oram. "You need to catch him. What if he comes back? And if he's killing off everyone who's owned the desk, Mr. Lao could be next. I should get downstairs."

Gage laid a soothing hand over Landry's. "Carson is with Mr. Lao, he's fine. Oram knows we're onto him now. He was disturbed when Carson came to find you and you escaped from him. He must assume that you ran straight to the cops. He also knows that we've realized there was something up with that particular piece of furniture. He'll connect the dots. He's not dumb."

Landry nibbled at a fingernail. "He knows we're together. He told me he was watching when I found the body so he must have seen you arrive. You gave me a hug. He doesn't know about the poison bottle though, does he? I mean, he doesn't know we have it. I pleaded ignorance and I think that's why he took me rather than killing me there and then — to question me about the bottle."

"You called it a *poison* bottle," Ellery observed.

"That's what Oram called it, though it wasn't obviously an antique pharmacist's bottle. It didn't have poison written on it or anything like that. In fact it looked more like a ladies' perfume bottle."

"It's already at the lab being tested. I always suspected Winterton's death wasn't from natural causes. His heart attack must have been brought on by ingesting some kind of poison." Ellery frowned. "I think we need to go ahead with the plan we worked out, Gage."

"Plan? What plan?" Landry glanced from Ellery to Gage. "Don't you two dare try to keep this from me. I was Landry-napped. I had to jump out of a moving car. That bastard hit me! Twice."

"You don't need to know the details, Landry. The most important thing here is to keep you safe. Oram, or whoever he is, is invested in finding the bottle. If he thinks there's a chance *you* didn't find it, he'll want to take another look at that desk."

"You're right. He didn't believe that I'd opened all the secret compartments, then Carson arrived and he had to go deal with him."

"So, we're going to draw him out."

"If you don't tell me, Gage, you'll be sleeping on the couch forever." Tears welled in Landry's eyes and his lip quivered.

"You may as well tell him, Gage," Ellery said. "He's going to find out anyway and I'd hate to think of you being denied access to that beautiful ass. That would be a true crime."

"Stop thinking about his ass."

"Stop thinking about my ass," Landry added.

Ellery fell about laughing.

"Fine, if it'll get Ellery onto a different topic, I'll tell you. We're going to make a change to Treasure Trove's window display."

Landry gaped. "You're going to put the secretaire in the store window?"

"Right where Oram can see it, yes."

"And he'll want to search it, so what? You're expecting him to break in?"

"Possibly. He may be desperate enough to try something bolder and come in when the store is open. Either way, we'll be waiting for him."

"And when you say 'we'…"

"Oram isn't familiar with Ellery, so he will man the store. You, Petey and Mr. Lao will be well clear. Ellery will be wired and will have a code word to call in the cavalry as soon as Oram makes a move."

"But that's not going to work, is it?" Landry huffed with impatience. "If Oram was watching when I found the body, who's to say he wasn't watching at other times. He was also here at least once already, remember. He knows I work here. He also knows I'm familiar with the desk. I need to be here. If you really want to draw him out, I need to look like a soft target and much as I hate to say it, James does not look sweet and innocent. He looks like he carries an eight-inch hunting blade in his underpants."

"More like eight and a half, almost nine on a good day." Ellery smirked.

"Shut up, Ellery. You are not..."

"Yes I am and once Petey finds out about this, you won't be able to stop him either." Landry folded his arms and adopted his most stubborn expression.

"Sweetheart..."

"Don't you 'sweetheart' me. Do you hear me using a safe word? I didn't think so. Now go get Petey and Carson so we can all talk about putting together a plan that might actually stand a chance of working."

Chapter Nineteen

The planning process turned into a team effort. They made the arrangements that day then the following morning, after an unsettled night, Mr. Lao and Prisha's dad brought the secretaire over from storage. Prisha's dad had a cup of coffee and a chat then went back to work, and Mr. Lao departed to take a short buying trip out of town. He wasn't very happy about leaving Landry and Petey in the store, but he understood that too much abnormal activity would look suspicious. As he no longer spent that much time in the store, it was better for him to be elsewhere.

Landry and Petey manhandled the desk into the window, having shifted Landry's chaise longue display to a different part of the store.

"Now, do we display it with the secret drawers open or closed?" Petey asked.

"I think we open one or two," Landry said. "I'll write on the sales card that the piece has several hidden compartments, which will entice people in. There's plenty of space in the window for me to demonstrate, if customers want a closer look, which I'm sure they will."

"Are you going to put a price on the card?"

"No. I think if anyone shows a lot of interest or says they want to buy it right away, we'll have to say it's reserved. Then we can say that if the buyer doesn't come through, we can let them know. It'll give us a good excuse to take people's details."

"Sounds good. Carson will be back from his shift soon. I wish he didn't have to work nights. I don't sleep well when he's not in bed with me. He's not very happy about this plan."

"Neither's Gage." Landry huffed. "They'll both have to deal."

Landry dressed the secretaire with some accessories from around the store. A leather-bound book, a gold-nibbed fountain pen and a bronze paperweight. "I know how you feel about sleeping alone. I'm the same, though Gage is rarely away all night. I guess it's something you get used to."

"Carson is talking about maybe getting into fire investigation. That would make his hours more regular. I think he's been inspired watching Gage at work"

"That must be fascinating," Landry said. "He'd be good at it, I'm sure. We're good investigators too though, aren't we?"

"We so are—the best. Do you think this Oram dude will show?"

"I hope so. Sounds weird, doesn't it, but I want this to be over and that can't happen until he's under arrest."

"Is that wire you're wearing uncomfortable?"

"Let's just say I'm glad I don't have a hairy chest. There's enough tape on me to wrap half a dozen parcels."

"Is Gage listening?"

"No. He and James had to make a show of going into the precinct. They're taking a circuitous route back then James will be in the kitchen at Mary's next door and Gage is going to hide out at the Eastern Emporium. Some of Gage's colleagues are listening in. I guess they're in a van somewhere. I didn't ask."

"I suppose we shouldn't talk about anything too kinky then?" Petey said, grinning.

"Oh, I don't know. I'm sure they'd enjoy an educational description of sounding or the technical developments in medical fetish equipment." Landry chuckled, imagining the expressions of the team listening nearby.

"You know they're gonna tell on you and Gage will spank you so hard."

"Oh, yes please!"

Over the next hour, Landry and Petey dealt with a steady stream of customers, most of whom asked questions about the secretaire. None of them bore any resemblance to Oram and Landry was beginning to wonder if he would show after all. In a pause between sales, he beckoned Petey over. "We need to act normal, and you haven't gone out for drinks yet. It's about time we had refreshments, don't you think?"

"Okay. Are you sure I should leave you here on your own though?"

"That's kind of the point of all this, isn't it? Take your time. We have to give Oram an opportunity to come in here when he thinks I'm vulnerable."

"Don't do anything dumb."

"As if. I'll need two jelly donuts and a triple shot, extra-foamy vanilla latte."

"On it. Take care, Lan."

Once Petey had left, Landry settled behind the cash desk and attempted to appear as normal as possible by scrolling through his phone rather than doing any work. When the bell over the door chimed, his heart jumped but the customer that walked in was a well-dressed woman. Landry fixed a smile on his face, disappointed. The woman, wearing a smart pantsuit, simple pink sweater and pearls, had a copper bob and mirrored sunglasses. She walked straight down the aisle toward him, high heels tapping on the wooden floor.

"Good morning, young man. I hope you can help me."

"I'll do my best." Landry slipped his phone onto the shelf beneath the cash register. "What are you looking for? Is it something in particular?"

"Jewelry I think, or something suitable for a lady's dressing table, perhaps. My brother is getting married, and I want to get a small engagement gift for my sister-in-law to be."

"I think something antique is a very personal, thoughtful gift," Landry said. "We have some lovely jewelry, a rather beautiful silver perfume bottle and a really nice walnut writing slope, inlaid with mother-of-pearl. Let me show you." Landry escorted his customer to the jewelry cabinet first where she seemed quite taken by a gold bracelet.

"It's simple, very tasteful," Landry said.

"I like it. I want something she'll wear. The perfume bottles are very pretty but I'm not sure she'd use them. I had one a bit like that once." She pointed out a small bottle with a pierced metal cap. "I'll take the bracelet. It's perfect and I don't believe in wasting time once I've made a decision."

"I'll wrap it for you," Landry said. "Feel free to take a look round."

He retreated to the cash desk to ring up the sale. "Dang, I forgot the box." He remembered that the bracelet had come in a velvet-lined box from the jeweler it had originally been purchased from in the 1940s. He'd tucked it at the back of the bottom shelf of the cabinet.

His customer was admiring the secretaire in the window. Landry fetched the box then went over to her. "It's interesting, isn't it?"

"It's fascinating," she said. "Would you mind showing me how it works?"

"Of course. Let me just take this box back to the cash desk." Landry placed the bracelet in its box then wrapped it in some tissue paper, pleased with a good sale. It was no hassle to spend some time with the lady—she might come back. As he strolled down the aisle, Landry noticed that the open sign was around the wrong way. "I'm sure I turned that over," he muttered, reaching for it.

"Please don't touch that."

Confused, Landry stared at his customer and straight down the barrel of a small, pearl-handled pistol. "I don't understand."

The woman approached him, yanked up his shirt then ripped the wire from his body. She crushed the microphone under the heel of her shoe.

"Ow! What the hell?" It dawned on Landry that he might be in trouble.

"Now, you will open every secret compartment on this desk, or I'll start putting bullets in you. This isn't a high-caliber pistol, but it can still do plenty of damage." She pushed the nose of the pistol into the hollow at the base of Landry's throat. "Be quick, I'm not stupid. I'm sure the police aren't far away, and it won't take them long to realize your mic is on the fritz."

Landry nodded, wondering how he could buy some time, but then realized that wasn't what he wanted to do. He needed to make sure this woman, whoever she was, was gone before Petey came back from the cafe.

Moving into the window, Landry began to open the drawers and cupboards on the secretaire. "Who are you?"

"If you need something done right, do it yourself." The woman's aim didn't waver. "I'm not about to give you my life story or tell you who I am. Give me the poison bottle and I'll be out of your life forever. You can go back to pottering around this quaint little store."

As he fumbled with catches and secret knobs, Landry took in as many details about the woman as he could. She spoke with an American accent but occasionally he caught a hint of something else. British, he thought. Her hair was dyed, light roots just showing through and her eyes were too blue. *Probably colored contacts.* "It isn't here, you know. The bottle. I already found it. The police have it." It was a calculated risk to give her the information, but Landry wanted her gone.

"You're lying!" The gun wavered.

"You have a gun in my face, I'm not lying." Landry stood back from the secretaire. "There you go, everything is open. The bottle was about three inches long. It had an ornate silver cap. I'd guess a late Victorian perfume bottle."

"Vinolia, 1892. Very rare and worth a fortune. He said you hadn't found it. Useless waste of space."

"He being Chet Oram." From the corner of his eye, Landry spotted Gage crossing the street. "You should leave. If you go now, you might just make it."

"I'm going to kill him. Slowly." The woman was less composed now. She flicked up the latch on the door, opened it and took a step back. Landry charged her and they both tumbled backward onto the street. The glass in the door exploded, showering them both with fragments. Reaching for the gun, Landry lost his footing. He landed hard, pulling the woman with him. There was a sharp retort as the gun went off. Landry screamed as warm liquid soaked his shirt.

"Landry!" Gage kicked the pistol away from where it had fallen on the sidewalk. He heaved the deadweight of the woman's body away from Landry. "Are you hurt?"

Landry batted Gage's hands away. "That's the one and only time I've ever been under a woman. Let me tell you, it was not fun. Is she dead?"

"Is she…? I don't know." Gage shifted his attention to the woman who was sprawled on the ground, one leg bent at a peculiar angle, her pants splattered with blood. One shoe had come off and was on its side, the heel broken. Gage felt for a pulse.

"She's alive. Looks like she shot herself in the leg."

People started to gather on the sidewalk. James Ellery appeared from the café, talking rapidly into a cell. A van screeched to a halt in the center of the street and more people spilled out. Landry lay where he was, debating his life choices, until Gage helped him to his feet.

* * * *

Twenty minutes later, Gage had gotten everyone around a table in Mary's café. Carson, who had returned from his night shift to scenes of chaos, sat next to Petey, who was pressed close to his side. Another five minutes and Petey would have been carrying drinks and pastries back to Treasure Trove. Sorrell sat nursing a hot chocolate, glancing every now and again at Ellery who was still on a call. Landry, poking his finger through a tear in another ruined garment, clutched his vanilla latte in his other hand. Gage laid a hand on Landry's knee to stop it bouncing.

"It's over, love. Take a breath."

"I have so many questions," Landry said. "Who was that woman? Where was Oram? Wasn't he the killer after all and in that case why did he kidnap me? I'm so confused." He downed a long swallow of coffee.

"I think I can help with that." Ellery pulled up another chair to join them. "The woman is Alicia Winterton, widow of the late Right Honorable Cecil Winterton. I've just had confirmation through from Interpol that Chet Oram is in fact one of Winterton's business partners, Duncan Farquhar. He's just been picked up at Schiphol airport in Amsterdam. He *was* the killer, Landry, of everyone except Winterton. That, I think we'll find, was the grieving widow."

"I still don't get it. Was she paying this Farquhar to kill people? Why did she get involved herself?"

"When we get to the bottom of this, Landry, I'd lay good money that this has all been about power and money. Control of Winterton's business interests and a huge insurance pay out."

Gage gave Landry's knee a gentle squeeze. "It always comes down to money and power."

"What about love?"

"I'm not sure people like these are capable of love," James said. "But I wouldn't be at all surprised to find that Alicia has been having an affair with Farquhar. If her husband found out, she would have been in danger of losing everything, as would his business partners. That's motivation for murder."

"So she killed him."

"Who better to know how to take advantage of his weak heart," James said. "Once any traces in the poison bottle are analyzed, we'll know for certain. She's definitely the mastermind behind all this. She couldn't risk trying to retrieve the bottle at the estate sale then it got away from her despite Farquhar's best efforts to catch up with it. I'd guess she knew Penton was the buyer and manipulated him into offering her lover a job. The shipment traveled by sea so Farquhar had time to be established in his role before the furniture arrived months later. What they didn't account for was the way the antiques trade works in this city."

"You guys sure are interesting to be around," Sorrell piped up.

"That's one way of putting it," Gage muttered. "I guess you'll be going back to the UK now then, Ellery. Two murderers caught. A huge amount of money saved for your employer. You'll be the golden boy."

"I'll be here a while. There are still a few odds and ends to finish up. I think I might be a tourist for a few days. Take in the sights of Seattle."

"I can show you around," Sorrell volunteered. "I still don't know what's happening with my job, so I have some free time."

"I want to get back to normal," Landry said. "The only weapon I want to get close to from now on is my feather duster."

"Good to hear." Gage scowled. "Sancha texted to let me know should be back in three days. She's made it clear she won't be helping me with any of the truckload of paperwork this case is going to generate."

"I need to call Mr. Lao to let him know what's going on," Landry said. "And I need to get the door glass fixed. Again."

"Better the door than you, love, though what in the ever-loving heck possessed you to tackle a woman with a gun?"

"She was going to get away. I saw you across the street. She might have shot you."

"Oh, love..." *How does he not realize he's the most important thing in my world?*

"Jesus Christ, someone bring me a bucket." Ellery made gagging noises. Gage gave him the finger.

"I can see what you're doing, Gage." Landry nuzzled his neck.

Gage ruffled his hair. "Don't care."

"So what now? I'd be quite happy to hibernate in bed for a month or so providing you're there with me."

"We carry on with our lives and soon"—Gage stroked Landry's throat—"I'm going to wrap my leather around your neck. Then you'll be stuck with me forever."

"That's adorable!" Sorrell gushed.

"That's...turning me on," Landry whispered. He glanced around the group to find every one of them smirking. "You heard that, huh?"

"How about we reconvene at Scorch tonight?" Gage suggested. "Ellery and I have to work. Landry, it's up to you whether you close the store. Carson needs to sleep."

"I do. I'll see if I can trade my shift tonight so I can join you at Scorch."

"I'm gonna keep the store open. With all the hullabaloo going on we'll have loads of rubberneckers in and Petey and I will relieve them of their hard-earned dollars."

"I'll come help," Sorrell offered. "I don't have anywhere else to be."

"That's settled then." Gage fixed Landry with a stern stare. "No getting into any more trouble, okay?"

"Would I, Sir?"

Ellery snorted. "Let's not go there."

"What he said." Gage shoved his chair back. "Behave, Lan. I mean it. Or you'll be over the spanking bench tonight."

"So not a disincentive, Sir." Landry blinked.

"And I'll let Ellery deliver the spanking."

Landry stared at him. "That's…your…you… Gonna go polish my halo now, Sir."

"You do that."

"You know, Gage, you'd have a great time if you and your boy ever decide to visit England. I can get you into a few exclusive places, like The Underground."

Gage had heard of the Underground. "That's the premiere BDSM club in England. They let you in?"

"Believe it or not," Ellery said, "not everyone thinks I'm an arsehole."

Gage snorted. "Who, your mom?"

"Oh, no. She totally does, a fact she reminds me of every Sunday when Tad and I go to dinner at her place."

The Ellery in Gage's mind wasn't the one who went to have a meal with his mother. He was the sarcastic, rude asshole that... He sighed. Maybe he needed to stop thinking in those terms. Ellery had been invaluable on the case, and —

"Plus, it would give me a chance to see your boy naked."

All Gage's goodwill went right out the window. "When we go out tonight, Landry, you'll be wearing something that covers every inch of skin, got it?"

"Yes, Sir."

Ellery grinned. "I can't wait."

Epilogue

Three months later…

Landry rubbed beeswax polish into a two-hundred-year-old piece of walnut and admired the grain. "This is a gorgeous blanket box, Petey. You want to take some pictures, put it on the website?"

"Sure. How about we drape those Welsh wool blankets you found over one end?"

"Good idea. You've got a real eye for this stuff."

"Thanks, it's fun."

"You could take a course, photography or design."

"Nah." Petey ducked his head. "I'm happy doing my thing for Treasure Trove."

"I forgot to tell you—we had gifts arrive from England this morning."

"From Ellery?"

"Yeah. He scored a huge bonus thanks to us."

"What did he send, a fruit basket?"

"Not quite. He gave Gage a rubber straitjacket to put me in and this fiendish anal hook contraption for predicament play."

"Wow! What did you get?"

"A leather jock and harness for Gage."

"Hot."

"Not what Gage said, I can tell you. There was also a thumb drive with a video of Ellery and Tad using similar items."

"No way!"

"Yes way. Gage sent Ellery a text, which from what I could see was a whole line of swear words."

"He's so gonna use that jacket though."

"Tonight." He licked his lips. "Can't wait." Landry put away his polish and cloth. "It'll take my mind off all the change going on around here. It's been a while since the ruby pendant and the coin went to auction. I can't believe how much they sold for." Landry hoped the collectors who had bought the treasure he'd found would get a great deal of pleasure from their purchases.

"It really was treasure. Are you sure about splitting the proceeds though? You found everything."

"Don't go there again. We've all talked about it and we agreed that when the treasure went to auction, we would all get a share. The profit goes four ways between you, me, Carson and Gage. No more arguing." At the mention of Gage, Landry touched the slim leather collar around his neck. He and Gage had chosen it together. Gage had fastened it in place in the privacy of their apartment. There had been candlelight, champagne, strawberries and an unforgettable night when Gage had revealed a penchant for inventive predicament play. Landry shivered happily at the memory. It was a night he'd never forget and since then Gage had been even more loving and attentive.

"Stop lusting after Gage!" Petey hip-checked him.

"Can't help it, he's lust worthy. He fucked me so hard this morning I thought the bed would break."

"He's perfect for you and so is Carson for me. I never thought we'd be able to afford our own place together and the coin has made that possible."

"You needed more space than the attic apartment and you said Carson had been saving too. I'm glad the coin helped. I'll miss you being my upstairs neighbor though."

"I won't be far away, and we'll even have a yard. That means we can grill! When Carson finishes his fire investigation training, he'll have more normal hours, which I can't wait for. You'll have Sorrell upstairs — he's itching to move in. His housemates are driving him crazy."

"I can't believe Treasure Trove is mine now, well, mine and Gage's. Mr. Lao didn't charge me anywhere near enough. I was so happy when Gage decided to put his share of the proceeds from the coin into the business too, but I never dreamed I'd be able to buy it outright. I own a building! I have to be responsible now."

"Mr. Lao wanted Treasure Trove to go to you and his family agreed, and I think Gage is the responsible one."

"Mr. L will still get to earn commission on anything he buys for stock. With you and Sorrell here, he'll be taking me on more buying trips so I can learn all his trade secrets."

"It's a shame Penton's Antiquarium has closed, but Sorrell said Penton's mom couldn't bear to keep the place on. You know Sorrell still hasn't got over working with a killer."

"Neither Farquhar nor Alicia Winterton will be getting out of prison for a long time. The two of them can write each other love notes from their cells. Sorrell has nothing to worry about—he was never a target, but I understand how uneasy it all made him feel."

"She was a piece of work, wasn't she? Kills off her husband, gets another to commit mass murder recovering the evidence. Why did she hide that bottle anyway?" Petey pursed his lips. "Seems like a dumb move."

"Gage confirmed what she told me—that the bottle is valuable. It had been an anniversary gift from her husband. She'd had the poison for some time, waiting for an opportunity to use it. She kept the bottle in plain sight on her dressing table. Once she'd used the poison, she hid the bottle where she thought no one would find it. She never intended to get rid of it, too greedy, but she didn't account for all the furniture being sold off to cover debts. She couldn't show special interest in that piece and had moved out of the castle while everything was assessed for sale. She didn't know until it was too late that it had been shipped abroad because who bought what at the sale was confidential."

"What a psycho."

"Cold, calculating and manipulative," Landry said. "The irony is that she could have gotten away with it if she hadn't been so greedy. The deaths in the UK meant James wouldn't give up the hunt. If they hadn't happened, Farquhar probably would have gotten the insurance payout. If someone found the bottle later, it would likely have been sold as an unexpected bonus."

"She had a rich husband, a castle… She still wasn't happy."

"According to Gage, Crowberry Castle was a money pit and a pre-nup meant she would never benefit from a divorce. Her husband was older so I'd bet she had a game plan in mind from the moment they met. Farquhar craved power too so he was prepared to do anything she told him to get it."

"But she lost patience."

"He was creating too many waves with the murders and taking too long to find the bottle." Landry shrugged. "She must have wondered if he was enjoying himself a bit too much. I wouldn't want to share a bed with someone who stabbed innocent people to death."

"I'll bet Gage is glad to be clear of the paperwork."

"He was very happy when Alicia Winterton was deported. He was at the point of hoping for a major crime spree. Sancha was so annoyed she missed everything, she had him filling in forms for weeks. I didn't tell you, did I…she's getting a promotion so she'll be Gage's boss as well as his partner." Landry cackled.

"Good for her!" Petey finished taking his pictures. "Sorrell is taking his own sweet time fetching drinks. You think he went all the way to the Coffee Bean instead of next door?"

"Wouldn't surprise me. He adores Tank. I should have a matchmaking side-line—I'd make a fortune."

The bell above the door chimed and Sorrell hustled down the aisle. "Sorry, sorry! It was rammed in there. Mary's giving discounts to all the garbage crews and those guys sure can eat. You know, Landry, if Mary gave out vouchers for Treasure Trove with meals we might get some new customers."

"Why don't you work up the idea?" Landry made grabby hands until Sorrell passed over his coffee.

"You mean it?" Sorrell bounced.

"Sure. Mary thinks you're cuter than me. Work your magic on her."

"Peppermint tea for you, Petey." Sorrell handed over the cup. "Cappuccino for me and I got brownies because Mary had just baked a new batch."

"Keep going like this, Sorrell, and I might have to give you a raise." Landry jammed a brownie in his mouth. "Oh, yum!"

"How's your…? Down there?" Sorrell flapped his hand in the direction of Landry's groin. Landry rolled his eyes. "The piercing has healed just fine, thank you, Sorrell."

"Tank likes piercings…"

"It's something you have to do for you, not just for him."

"I think it's hot too," Sorrell whispered.

Petey snickered. "But does Tank want to…?"

"Petey!" Landry yelled. "Don't you dare…"

"Does he want to what?" Sorrell asked. "You have to tell me now."

"Run a chain from the guiche to a penis plug."

"We're no longer friends!" Landry put down his coffee, grabbed a feather duster and chased Petey around the store.

"A what, now?" Sorrell shouted.

The chaos was interrupted by the arrival of a customer whom Sorrell went to help. Petey got to work on the website and Landry wandered to the front of the store to look out onto the rain-soaked street.

He smiled. "My kind of normality." He couldn't help but wonder how long it would last.

Want to see more from this author? Here's a taster for you to enjoy!

The Retreat: Finding Him
L.M. Somerton

Excerpt

Carey Hoffman stepped out of the air-conditioned limousine into the burning heat of a Palm Springs summer's day. The air shimmered, and he half-expected to see a mirage in the distance along with a camel train and a bunch of wandering nomads. The sun's intensity made the greenery around him all the more astounding. Extensive, manicured lawns stretched to either side of the sweeping drive and in front of him stood the biggest, most palatial house he'd ever seen. He could only imagine how much watering all that lush grass would need.

"It's enormous." Pure white, the sun reflecting off the building's curved walls was blinding. Carey slipped on his sunglasses to reduce the combined glare of the sun and the paintwork. He couldn't decide whether he liked the property or not. There was no doubt that it was extravagant and no question it was unique. "Probably designed by some celebrity architect for an extortionate fee," Carey muttered. "It must be worth a small fortune."

"I kind of like the smooth lines, it's all curves, no harsh edges." Alistair, Carey's partner and submissive, joined him, slipping his hand into Carey's. "It doesn't come across as ostentatious as the McMansions you see in California. It's understated, restrained somehow."

"That's your artistic eye at work, love. There's way too much white for my liking. What's wrong with a bit of color? Or at the very least a shade of white that isn't…misty cloud or curdled milk or something. There are whole pages of so-called whites on paint charts, though they mostly look the same to me."

Alistair gave him a gentle smile. "The heat's getting to you, isn't it, Sir?"

"How do people around here not combust? This place is like a furnace—I feel like I'm desiccating just standing here. What I wouldn't give for a dose of London drizzle right now and that's not something I ever thought I'd say."

"We're English. Our bodies are not equipped for more than two hot days a year—and by hot, I mean low eighties, not high nineties. Everything here seems to be air-conditioned to the point of frigidity, and I'm sure the house will be, too, once we get inside. You'll be much happier then."

"It's entirely your fault we're here, you know that? Now you're a famous photographer, everyone wants a piece of you. Even multimillionaires. A personal invite from Taylor Denman is not to be sniffed at." Carey gave Alistair a kiss to demonstrate his pride. "I'm so proud of you love, even if I am being fried alive."

"Do you wish I'd turned down the invitation?" Alistair gazed at him anxiously. "I would have if you'd asked me to."

"Absolutely not! Ignore me, sweetheart. The heat's making me fractious. I'm very glad you accepted the invitation and I'm intrigued to meet Mr. Denman since he sponsored your exhibition in San Francisco. It was an enormous success. I've never seen so many sold stickers at a show before and it wouldn't surprise me if he bought some of the pictures himself. You worked really hard to get everything set up, the launch was wonderful but exhausting. Mr. Denman's offer to spend a few days at one of his hotels was a perfect way to end our trip so you could hardly turn down an invitation to meet him in person. It's a small price to pay for an all-expenses paid stay in the best hotel in Palm Springs."

They walked toward the house, glittering quartz gravel crunching beneath their shoes.

"I have to confess I'm a little nervous." Alistair gripped Carey's hand tighter.

"There's no need to be. I'm here and I'll take care of you."

"You always do." Alistair smiled, and Carey's breath hitched. Alistair was beautiful, the sun glinting on his blond hair, his skin showing a hint of tan from several weeks in the sun.

"And I always will." There was no doubt about that in Carey's mind. Taking care of Alistair was the single most fulfilling part of his existence.

As they approached the huge front door of the property, it swung open. Carey expected to see a butler or maybe a personal assistant, but it was Taylor Denman himself who stood waiting for them. Carey recognized him from pictures he'd seen in the press. Taylor was casually dressed in jeans and a light blue shirt, the sleeves rolled up to reveal tanned arms and the curl of a tattoo. He was a striking man, about Carey's age, his chestnut hair starting to silver at the temples. A trace of stubble shaded his jaw, and there were laughter lines around his eyes.

"Welcome, gentlemen. I'm so glad you were able to make the trip from San Francisco." Taylor stepped forward with a welcoming smile.

"Thank you for inviting us, Mr. Denman," Alistair said. "We're so happy to meet you."

"Call me Taylor. You're Alistair of course, I know you from your catalog picture, so this must be Carey." He shook hands with Carey first, then with Alistair. "Come inside, it's hotter than the surface of the fucking sun out here, excuse my language."

Alistair giggled. "You and Carey are going to get along really well."

"I thought it was only us rain-soaked Brits who couldn't handle it," Carey said, following Taylor into the icy-cool interior of his home. "I'm melting."

"I was born in Canada. Alberta. I don't think I'll ever get used to the heat, but my business interests make having a home here convenient. I keep an apartment in New York but I thought you'd appreciate a few days here in Palm Springs after the bustle of San Francisco. It's a lot more relaxing than The Big Apple."

"We certainly appreciate it," Carey said, gazing around the entrance hall. "It's rare that we get to spend a few days alone together, and the exhibition was a little frantic. Thanks to you it drew a lot of attention." He was impressed by the cool colors and sleek minimalist design. The area managed to be welcoming even though the cathedral-like ceiling height could have made it intimidating.

His eye was drawn to a wall displaying a single large picture. Carey smiled. It was one of Alistair's photographs, blown up to huge proportions. The original was one of Carey's favorites. It showed a vast, ancient oak, standing alone in a rural landscape at twilight, its gnarled limbs outlined against the sky. A silhouette of a fox was just visible at its base. Ironically, it hadn't taken hours of patient waiting for an animal to appear. He and Alistair had driven out to the Chiltern hills one afternoon and had been taking a stroll after an early dinner at a nearby restaurant. Alistair, his photographer's instinct always active, had lifted his camera and taken the snap after spotting movement. He hadn't even known it was a fox until he'd looked at the digital image. It had been pure luck that the picture had come out so well. It had sold at a London gallery, but the buyer had remained anonymous.

Alistair edged a little closer to Carey's side, blushing. "Now you know what happened to the picture," Carey said with a chuckle.

"I was curious," Alistair admitted. "Anonymous buyers are intriguing."

"The original is in my study," Taylor said. "I had this print made specifically for this space, and you have no idea how many compliments it draws. I'm loath to praise your work in public, Alistair because it never fails to increase competition for the pictures I want to buy. I'm a covetous man—I want the best for myself."

"I'm so flattered. The picture certainly suits this space. I'm glad it went to someone who appreciates it."

"Well, I've added several more to my collection thanks to the San Francisco exhibition. Shameless self-interest got me involved and as sponsor I got first pick, which caused huge annoyance to several acquaintances. An added bonus, I admit." He grinned, mischief glittering in his eyes. "But I have to confess that it's not the reason I've invited you both here. I'm afraid I have been somewhat dishonest. Of course, I sponsored the exhibition for absolutely genuine reasons, but over the last year things have come to light that I think you may be able to help me with. A personal matter."

"You have my attention," Carey said. "Does this have something to do with Alistair's photography skills?"

"No. Actually, Carey, it's you that I think can help. Let's go sit in the sun room. I have light snacks set out in there, and cold drinks. We can relax and you can hear me out."

Carey exchanged a curious glance with Alastair who shrugged, apparently unconcerned by the mystery. They both followed Taylor through the house pausing to admire the pictures and sculptures that were displayed everywhere.

The sun room proved to be constructed entirely of glass but managed to remain ice-cold. Several comfortable loungers surrounded a low glass table and there was a magnificent view of the sweeping grounds. Carey guessed that the hint of glittering water in the distance must be a pool.

They settled into their seats, Carey and Alistair next to each other, Taylor opposite them. Taylor offered them a selection of drinks. Alistair opted for chilled mango juice while Carey accepted a light beer, mirroring Taylor's choice. On the table sat several platters of cold finger food, which was tempting but Carey wanted to hear what Taylor had to say before switching his attention to snacks.

"How do I start?" Taylor leaned forward, steepling his fingers.

"I find it's always best to be direct," Carey said.

"Perhaps the best way for me to introduce this subject is to mention that we have a mutual acquaintance." Taylor stared at the view rather than meeting Carey's eyes. "A close friend of mine, Lorcan Wilder."

Alistair reached for Carey's hand. Carey took it and gave it a comforting squeeze. "Lorcan is a good friend of mine too. How do you know him?"

"We met through various business dealings before he sold his company, and now I'm involved in some of his philanthropic endeavors. I contribute to a number of the projects he supports through his foundation but that's not why I mentioned his name. Lorcan told me all about his stay at The Retreat and how he met his Rowan, who I have to say is the sweetest young man. He's perfect for Lorcan."

"They are very well suited," Carey said, not bothering to conceal his curiosity. "But what's your interest in The Retreat? I have to admit I would never have guessed that was what you wanted to talk about."

"I know I can trust your discretion," Taylor said, finally meeting Carey's gaze. "And for that reason I'm going to give you a bit of context. My wife died a long time ago, but she and I enjoyed a relationship that was not always vanilla. I'm not completely ignorant of the BDSM lifestyle, though Anya and I never played outside of the privacy of our own home. I've also known Lorcan for a long time, he knows I like to play occasionally."

"You understand that The Retreat only caters for men?" Carey said.

"Yes, I do." Taylor chuckled. "I'm sorry, I'm usually more direct than this. I'm not interested in a stay at The Retreat for myself. It's for my son, Zac."

Alistair squeezed Carey's fingers, and Carey gave him a nod to let him know he could speak. "Mr. Denman, Taylor, are you saying you want to book a stay at a BDSM retreat for your son?"

"I suppose I am, Alistair."

"Forgive me for saying so, but that's rather unusual."

"I realize it's rather a strange request, but I can assure you it's in his best interests."

"That's so cool." Alistair beamed. "The Retreat is an amazing place."

"We are a little biased, though," Carey admitted. "Okay, a lot biased."

"I can assure you that Lorcan has the same opinion otherwise we wouldn't be talking. I've taken his advice on this. I know this is…unusual but I'm extremely fortunate in having a very close relationship with Zac. He's always been very open with me, and I'm proud that he feels able to be that way. I'm not sure whether I knew he was gay before he did or if it was the other way round, but he never had to come out to me. I've always been as supportive as possible and encouraged him to be open when he felt he could." Carey nodded his approval. "However, being my son comes with a unique set of issues. Over the years there have been several threats against Zac. Let me be clear, that's got nothing to do with his sexuality, it's to do with my money and the fact that he's my only heir. Zac has always had to deal with understanding that he's at risk of being kidnapped. He's recently finished college but his roommate was also his bodyguard. Other than the Internet, he's had very little chance to explore the way he tells me he feels."

"And how is that? Does he think he's a Dom?" Carey asked.

Taylor shook his head. "The opposite. He takes after his mother. He has her looks and her submissive streak. He tells me that he wants to explore that further. He's an adult, he can do as he pleases but he wants my blessing, and I want him safe."

"Forgive me," Carey said, "I'm still not quite seeing what you need from us."

"It's not my intention to be obtuse. I want to help Zac find a Dom in a safe, protected environment. He can't go to clubs or leather bars—he'd be recognized. Don't get me wrong, I have no issue with reputation here, though Zac deserves his privacy. It's a security problem. I want him to have the opportunity to experience submission and potentially meet someone he can connect with in the same profound way that I did with his mother. The catch is that longer term, his Dom will also need to be his protector. I need a good man to keep my boy safe, Carey. That's what I want you to help me with, though I don't expect a short stay at The Retreat to solve everything of course—just get Zac on the start line as it were."

Alistair sighed. "That's so amazing. Zac is very lucky to have such good relationship with you."

"Alistair's relationship with his father was nowhere near so healthy," Carey said, repressing a shudder at the memory of the evil that man had committed. "But you realize, Taylor, that I can't countenance going anywhere with this unless it's with Zac's full agreement."

"Of course, and that's why I'd like you to meet him. He's fully on board with the plan, I can assure you. You can come in now, Zac."

Carey hadn't noticed the door that Zac came through, until it opened, it was so cleverly concealed in a mirrored panel. The young man that strolled across the room to join them was visually striking and clearly Taylor's son. His wavy hair was a shade darker than his father's, his cheekbones were sharper and his lips fuller. It was his eyes that caught Carey's attention. The unusual shade of pale green, framed by dark lashes, was arresting. Zac's mother must have been an exceptionally attractive woman.

"Zac, come and meet Mr. Hoffman and his famous photographer partner, Alistair. I need you to convince Mr. Hoffman that I'm not trying to pimp you out," Taylor said, rising to give his son a hug.

"You're not?" Zac grinned as they pulled apart and laughed when Taylor gave him a light cuff. "Okay, you're not!" He turned to Carey. "It's a pleasure to meet you, Mr. Hoffman. My friend Rowan thinks you have magical powers when it comes to matchmaking." Zac's voice was deep and melodic. He spoke with quiet confidence, but Carey could tell he was nervous.

"It's a pleasure to meet you, Zac. This is my...partner, Alistair," Carey said.

Alistair rolled his eyes. He pulled his shirt down to show the narrow leather collar around his neck. "I'm his *submissive* partner. If you're friends with Rowan, then I guess you understand how that works."

"It's a great pleasure, Alistair. Dad moons over your pictures constantly. He's quite the fan boy."

"Zac!" Taylor protested, "Stop giving away my secrets."

Alistair blushed. "I'm a bit in awe. Can we get back to talking about submission—it's a much easier topic?"

Carey gave Alistair a fond look. "So, you're hoping to learn more about the lifestyle, Zac?"

"I want to. I know this whole plan must seem crazy but...well, it *is* kind of crazy, I suppose. I want to find out what sort of submissive I am. I want to meet different men in a way that doesn't send my dad into a tailspin. When Lorcan told us about The Retreat, everything fell into place, and it seemed like the perfect solution."

"We don't run a dating agency," Carey said. "What we can do is provide Dominants for you to play with, different men with differing skill sets depending on what you think you might like to try. Are you a masochist? Do you enjoy pain? Do you want to be humiliated or forced?"

"I don't know!" Zac's face pinked. "I just know I want to find out." He scuffed the toe of his sneaker against the polished floor. "Can you help me?"

"Of course we will!" Alistair jumped to his feet then pulled Zac into a hug. "Won't we, Sir?"

Carey knew there and then that he had no choice in the matter. "Something you'll soon realize, Zac, is that submissives hold all the power in our world." Carey shook his head.

Alistair giggled as he returned to Carey's side. "Well, we *will* help, won't we? You love a challenge, Sir."

"If you say so, love." Taylor seemed bemused, Zac hopeful. "There are details to be hammered out, but yes," Carey said. "The Retreat should be able to fulfill what you need to a certain extent. I can't guarantee you'll meet anyone you want to make a lasting connection with but I'll discuss your case with Luke Redding, the manager at The Retreat, and he'll be in touch. There's an extensive waiting list, so I don't know how long it will be before…"

"I made the reservation some time ago," Taylor said. "Under a false name. Zac and I decided to wait until he'd finished college, but we've been planning this for a while. The booking is for two weeks and begins at the start of September. I trust that will give you adequate time to prepare?"

Carey wasn't often surprised, and he didn't let it show on his face, but he was impressed by Taylor's forethought. He was also a little concerned about the timescale. "That will be fine. We'll look forward to welcoming Zac in September."

"Excellent. Now that's agreed, perhaps Zac could loan Alistair some swim shorts and show him the pool, while I take you to admire my wine cellar? I don't get the chance to show it off often enough, and Lorcan tells me you know your vintages. Now our business is done, it would be very nice to relax with new friends, if you don't mind staying a while."

Carey glanced at Alistair who was bouncing with excitement. "That sounds perfect." Alistair and Zac were already moving. "You can tell me all about Zac. Any insights you can give me will be helpful." Carey fancied that Taylor's smile was warmer, less tense, than before. "And I'm sure he'll give Alistair all kinds of useful information."

"I'll do my best, Carey, and perhaps you can help me choose an appropriate bottle to go with supper. My driver will take you back to your hotel this evening."

Carey relaxed. Good company, food and wine would be the perfect end to a surprising day. There would be time back in England to consider how best to meet Zac's unusual needs.

About the Author

Lucinda lives in a small village in the English countryside, surrounded by rolling hills, cows and sheep. She started writing to fill time between jobs and is now firmly and unashamedly addicted.

She loves the English weather, especially the rain, and adores a thunderstorm. She loves good food, warm company and a crackling fire. She's fascinated by the psychology of relationships, especially between men, and her stories contain some subtle (and some not so subtle) leanings towards BDSM.

L.M. Somerton loves to hear from readers. You can find her contact information, website details and author profile page at https://www.pride-publishing.com

PUBLISHING

Sign up for our newsletter and find out about all our
romance book releases, eBook sales and promotions,
sneak peeks and FREE romance books!